D1239369

Keeping House

SUNY series,

WOMEN WRITERS IN TRANSLATION

Marilyn Gaddis Rose
editor

Keeping House

a novel in recipes

Clara Sereni

Translated from the Italian by
Giovanna Miceli Jeffries
and Susan Briziarelli

STATE UNIVERSITY OF NEW YORK PRESS

Cover Art: Watercolor "Keeping House" by Brian Peterka.
Illustrations on pages 21, 25, 37, 67, 97, 107, 117, and 131 by Brian Peterka.

Excerpts from "Caring and Nurturing in Italian Women's Theory and Fiction: A Reappraisal," in *Feminine Feminists: Cultural Practices in Italy*, edited by Giovanna Miceli Jeffries, are reprinted with permission from the University of Minnesota Press.

Excerpts from "La tensione civile nella narrativa di Clara Sereni," in *Studi in onore di Umberto Mariani: da Verga a Calvino*, edited by Anthony G. Costantini and Franco Zangrilli, are reprinted with permission from Edizioni Cadmo.

Published by
STATE UNIVERSITY OF NEW YORK PRESS
ALBANY

© 2005 State University of New York

For information, address State University of New York Press, 194 Washington Avenue, Suite 305, Albany, NY 12210-2384

Production, Laurie Searl
Marketing, Fran Keneston

Library of Congress Cataloging-in-Publication Data

Sereni, Clara, 1946–
    [Casalinghitudine. English]
    Keeping house : a novel in recipes / Clara Sereni ; translated by Giovanna Miceli Jeffries and Susan Briziarelli.
        p. cm. — (SUNY series, women writers in translation)
    Includes bibliographical references.
    ISBN 0-7914-6479-2 (hardcover : alk. paper)
    1. Cookery, Italian—Fiction. I. Miceli Jeffries, Giovanna. II. Title. III. Series.

PQ4879.E718C3713 2004
853'.914—dc22
                                                          2004015111

10   9   8   7   6   5   4   3   2

Contents

Preface   vii

Acknowledgments   ix

Translators' Note   xi

Introduction   1

1   For a Baby   21

2   Appetizers   25

3   First Courses   37

4   Second Courses   67

5   Eggs   97

6   Vegetables   107

7   Sweets   117

8   Preserving   131

Notes   145

Works Cited   149

Preface

Once, for a presentation of *Casalinghitudine* in Tuscany, the organizers had the idea of pairing my talk with a glass of good wine and a sampling of the dishes from the book. Naturally I, too, partook of this, discovering to my surprise that the dishes were all good, but all different from how I knew them. This was because the Tuscan beans were not the same ones I used to buy in Rome, because distances of just a few kilometers make for different cheeses and cold cuts, and, above all, because cooking is not an exact science. My pinch of salt is different from yours, my idea of "a little oil," is certainly so subjective that it does not allow exact replication. But I, too, when cooking my "seven grain soup" in another country, came up with an entirely new taste, even though I had made it with my own hands, my amounts, and my methods. With the passing of time, needs and recipes change. Indeed, in my experience, in the years since the book first appeared in Italy, almost none of the dishes have remained exactly the same. Everything flows, everything changes: how could food remain the same? The number of people around the table changes, the availability of money and time changes, our physical and creative needs change. If I had kept my cooking more rigid, my life would have stopped as well, frozen, blocked.

Because the nice thing about cooking (the only truly creative act of housekeeping) is just that inexactness, with its gray area that allows space for invention, modification, appropriation. For everyone, knowledge and memory are at play each time, as they are in this book, whose placement I imagine somewhere between living room and kitchen, with its cover made richer by the presence of the occasional floury or greasy fingerprints. Therefore, I explicitly authorize the reader to use it simply as an outline, as technical support to retrace one's own story, one's own roots, the scents and flavors that guide us (and pursue us) from past to present. And perhaps with the strength that comes to us from memory it will be possible for us to face the future with greater confidence.

Clara Sereni, Perugia (Italy), January 2005
Trans., Susan Briziarelli

Acknowledgments

A heartfelt thank you to my family for their encouragement, support, and resources while working on this project, especially Tom and Carla.

G. Miceli Jeffries

I am grateful to Mary Moog for her careful and insightful reading of the translation, and to the University of San Diego for its support. A special thank you to my children, Chiara and Matteo, for their patience.

Susan Briziarelli

Translators' Note

Translating *Keeping House* was motivated by our firm conviction of the importance of this book in Italian literature and culture. We feel that the book is a fascinating and well-written documentation of a crucial time in Italian time and history, and should be made available to an English-speaking readership.

Keeping House posited numerous challenges and major decisions to the translators. Our initial challenge regarded the recipes themselves. Unlike those in conventional cookbooks, Sereni's recipes are discursive rather than prescriptive, and rendering them faithfully in English was not always easy. A "handful" (*pugno*) or a "bit" (*po'*) are subjective measures that are understandable in English as well, and we wanted to leave them unchanged, in order to retain the familiar tone established by the author. Other measures commonly used in Italy, however, do not have equivalents in English and, indeed, can be misleading. The word *cucchiaino* means small spoon, but is actually much smaller than the American teaspoon. *Bicchierino* and *bicchiere* literally translate into "small glass" and "glass" respectively, but are still approximate measures compared to the exactness of the American cup. Of course, leaving these measurements with their original designations would have been a more desirable and poetic choice. But we also knew, as we read and reread the text and found ourselves sampling some of the recipes, that a more exact measurement was preferable and useful.

Sereni's striking and unusual prose style presented a second challenge to the translation. Much of her style relies on the creation of an almost musical phrase through the unconventional use of punctuation, pauses, suspensions, and abrupt endings.

Her sentences can often be formulaic, like the recipes, chained in nominal constructions where emotions are almost palpable, with sparing inflected verbs and a preference for the encompassing quality of the indefinites, both as grammatical subjects and objects of the verbs. These mechanisms did not produce the same effect in English, and we found ourselves faced with the task of finding a balance between retaining the authenticity of Sereni's style and making it work in English.

A final issue was that of the author's assumption of the reader's familiarity with a specific historical and cultural background and context. Throughout the book, the informed Italian reader encounters names, dates, locations, and brand names that are not necessarily familiar to the non-Italian reader. Figures such as Pietro Nenni, leader of the Italian Socialist Party, and Leopold Sedar Senghor, the Senegalese intellectual and political leader who developed the concept of "negritude," appear along with icons of the Italian and European cinema, such as Dino Risi and Rainer Werner Fassbinder. The name of the fashion designer Luisa Spagnoli is another household name that is a signifier, for every Italian, of taste, elegance, and understatement. To document every one of these cultural references would have required numerous notes, and would have thus drastically altered the flow of the novel. We limited the documentation and clarifications to what we considered most germane to the reader's understanding of the book. We also made the decision to give names in their entirety rather than the last name only, as Sereni more familiarly does.

We trust and hope that the richness and uniqueness of *Keeping House* will surface in this translation, and that readers will enjoy and 'taste' this literary and culinary Italian product.

Introduction

Giovanna Miceli Jeffries

Per graduare giustamente i vari ingredienti non c'è che
un modo: assaggiare, assaggiare, assaggiare.

There is only one way to adjust ingredients:
taste, taste, taste.

—Clara Sereni, *Casalinghitudine*

Keeping House (*Casalinghitudine*) is a contemporary classic of
Italian literature. Right after its publication in 1987, it quickly
became a cult favorite for a generation of Italian women in the
late 1980s and 1990s. Structured around 105 recipes, *Keeping
House* is an autobiographical novel in which food is simultaneously the working metaphor and the material product in the narrator's journey of self-discovery and subject formation. Published
two years before Laura Esquivel's hugely popular *Like Water for
Chocolate*, *Keeping House* is among the pioneers of what has
become a significant narrative trend over the last two decades. In
the eighties, Nora Ephron's *Heartburn* dispensed two dozen
recipes as the female protagonist went through the ups and downs
of life as a pregnant woman married to an unfaithful husband.
The now famous key lime pie incident certainly invited humorous
reflection by readers and replication of the recipe. (I personally
became acquainted with this illustrious American dessert while

reading the novel.) In Elizabeth Ehrlich's *Miriam's Kitchen: A Memoir*, recipes are the conveyors of memory and bonds, and allow for the reaffirmation of cultural heritage, a process that also informs Helen Barolini's *Festa. Recipes and Recollections of Italian Holidays*. Barolini's book is a memoir journeying through seasonal celebrations of food and customs rooted in local anthropology and the author's life history between two cultures and two countries. Food marks the coming of age of food writer and author Ruth Reichl in her memoir *Tender at the Bone*, and mediates her passion for the good story and the poignant humor of her memories. Raised in the adventurous, unpredictable kitchen of her mother, at a young age Ruth exhibits a precocious sense of observation and a keen relationship to the emotional role of food and its mediating power, much like young Clara in *Keeping House*. In more recent years, even culinary mysteries—a subgenre of its own—are becoming progressively popular, promising a variety of thrillers and tastes.[1]

The original Italian title, *Casalinghitudine*, which the author created by combining *casalinga* (homemaker or housewife) with the sum of *abitudine, solitudine, negritudine* (habit, solitude, negritude), is now found as a neologism in the Italian dictionary of new words. A book that has never been out of print, *Keeping House* established the author as a major contemporary and original voice, a voice in which a generation of women who were active protagonists of the struggles and actions of the late sixties' protest movements could recognize themselves. Even the mothers of these women could recognize themselves in their unresolved, albeit never contested, relation with the home as both sanctuary and prison.

Born in Rome in 1946, Clara Sereni lives in Perugia with her husband and their son. From 1995 to 1997, Sereni occupied the charge of deputy mayor of Perugia, and was responsible for the city's social policies and libraries. During her tenure, she was very active and committed to promoting policies to improve women's lives. Particularly successful was Project Woman, an educational program designed to train women to run for political positions to ensure fair representation in local and national government.

Another initiative Sereni was devoted to was the Time Bank project, a system of banking volunteer hours, which could be "cashed
out" by participants when needed. Sereni also toughened codes
against sexual molestation and strove for local application of the
Italian national law regulating time schedules (affecting store
opening and closing times and public transportation schedules)
and other services in the city that allow for a better quality of life
for women and families. Sereni is also a regular opinions colum-
nist for *L'Unità* and *il manifesto*, major leftist Italian newspapers,
as well as for other national papers and magazines. She is the
president of the City of the Sun,[2] a foundation whose mission is
to create projects for developmentally disabled people and to edu-
cate the public, because, in her words, "only in a better society
can its weaker members find their own place, and a chance for a
life worth living."[3]

Two of Sereni's books have been finalists for the prestigious
Strega Prize: *Manicomio primavera* (1989) [Bedlam Spring], and *Il
gioco dei regni* (1993) [The Game of the Kingdoms], this last one
translated into both Hebrew and French. *Passami il sale* (2002)
[Pass the Salt], has been awarded three Italian literary prizes: the
Carlo Levi, Pisa, and Grinzane-Cavour prizes. Other books by
Sereni are: *Sigma epsilon* (1974), *Mi riguarda* (co-author, 1994) [I
Care], *Eppure* (1995) [And Yet], *Si può* (co-author, 1996) [One
Can], *Taccuino di un'ultimista* (1998) [Notes from the Side of the
Least], and *Le merendanze* (2004) [The Brunchers].

However, it is her seminal novel *Keeping House*, with its original structure and its articulation of private and public life that
has defined Sereni's place in cultural history and in Italian
women's writing. Recipes and food are the ordering and guiding
principles of *Keeping House*. Chapters are named after courses in
a complete meal and follow the order of a typical cookbook:
"Appetizers," "First Courses," "Second Courses," "Eggs," "Vegetables," "Sweets." The first and the last chapters, "For a Baby"
and "Preserving," are appropriately the symbolic posts, life lines
of three generations, food to nurture the narrator's new baby, to
start new life at the beginning of the book, and food to preserve
with memories that will carry on through generations. Guided by
the "scent" of recipes and ingredients highlighting the narrator's

journey toward self-discovery and understanding, the reader of *Keeping House* navigates through a complex web of growth experiences that are not linear or sequential—the narrator's most recent life experience is told in the first chapter, "For a Baby"— but rather episodic and cyclical, as the memory of a particular dish unwinds a segment of life that acquires particular significance and sheds supplemental light on what comes before or after in the narration. Familiar characters reappear and change, while others disappear. Food marks the coming of age of the protagonist-narrator and mediates between the personal and the public while simultaneously assembling and composing an otherwise fragmented reality made up of mixtures of various temporal dimensions and cultural genealogies. Readers will find and recognize Italian history and culture with the same familiarity as the ingredients of the recipes. The major events of Italy's cultural and political history in the twentieth century provide the moving background and stage for the narrator's life: fascism and antifascism, the early years of the young Italian republic, the politics and culture of the Italian left, the group life of the sixties and seventies, and the retreat into privacy in the eighties. All this exists side by side with the nonverbal language of food and recipes, and, more than that, of food prepared, served, and eaten before, after, and around public and private histories.

In *Keeping House*, food and recipes fulfill multiple functions and mediate the narrator's roles of daughter, mother, and wife while marking major personal and public landmarks: there are food and recipes for caring and being cared about; for learning to cook; for learning to become independent; for comforting oneself and others in hard times; controversial food that questions principles and positions; food for making up and repairing torts; food for celebrating political and private moments; food for rituals, for finding one's roots; food as a collective effort; food as a critique of social classes.

The late Gian Paolo Biasin writes that, in a novel, food "is a cognitive tool used to outline the problematic relations among subject, nature and history" ("Italo Calvino in Mexico: Food and Lovers, Tourists and Cannibals," 74). As a formidable metonym of the world, the representation of food in fiction brings various dimensions into play, all interacting and concurrent to the "read-ability of the world"[4]: anthropological, sociological, political, and cultural. There is something both historical and ahistorical in the representation of food in the literary text; on the one hand, food and its preparation carves out the context and the characters in their cultural, historical milieu; on the other hand, food contributes an unfashionably "eternal," durable quality to the story. In a similar way, Elio Vittorini splendidly captures the character of Concezione, planted in her kitchen in men's shoes, roasting herrings, a timeless figure having "nothing to do with history" (*Conversation in Sicily*, 148).[5]

Across cultures, recipes and food appear, especially in women's novels, to recreate personal histories, to reconnect, as Mexican author Laura Esquivel observes, "the self with the elements of the universe" and thus help us "come to understand our past and ourselves."[6] In the novel *Sassafras, Cypress and Indigo* by African American author Ntozake Shange, recipes reveal and differentiate the personalities of the three protagonist sisters, their lifestyles, and common background. At the same time, Shange sees recipes as a validation of women's traditional role as caretakers, and of the time they spend cooking for and feeding others.[7] Still, to the educated female Ph.D. in William Least Heat-Moon's *PrairyErth*, who chooses to run a small town café in the middle of the Kansas plains and cook for a living, the provision of food provides the opportunity for her to see her femaleness differently; her feminism is "connected with other people, not just with feminists" (130).[8]

When I asked Clara Sereni what cooking and the preparation of food represented to her, she commented that her interest in cooking and food is as a form of caring. Following the premature death of her mother when Clara was still a child, raised in an unconventional household made up of a grandmother, a great aunt, a stepmother, four sisters vastly spaced in age, and an emotionally distant father, Sereni does not make it a secret that perhaps she did not feel cared for as she was growing up and that she always craved affection and cuddling.[9] Food and the rituals accompanying its preparation, particularly preserving and canning, allowed her to bond with the adults around her and reaffirm her Jewish roots.

Sereni grew up in Rome in a Jewish Italian family, whose members had different levels of religious observance. Her father was the late Emilio Sereni, one of the writers of the postwar Italian Constitution and an executive in the Italian Communist Party. He held positions both as senator and representative in the Italian Parliament and, as a scholar and organizer, was very involved in agricultural and land policies. Appointed in the early fifties to head the party's cultural commission, for a short period he steered the policy of the left toward the preservation of Italy's national culture to resist America's growing influence. An antifascist intellectual who in his youth, with his older brother Enzo, had embraced the ideals of zionism (later rejected because of contradictions with his orthodox Marxism), Emilio Sereni was imprisoned by the fascist regime and lived in exile until the end of World War II. History and politics run throughout Clara Sereni's maternal and paternal blood. A Marxist atheist, Sereni's father was not observant, and the person most responsible for bringing her up with a sense of Jewish tradition and lore was her great aunt who was very involved in the Jewish Roman community. Through her especially, young Clara enjoyed days of Jewish observances ritually celebrated with special foods and elegant table settings. As an adult and a mother, Sereni makes a deliberate choice to reclaim her Jewish roots, in the process of composing what she calls her "mosaic-like" identity. After undertaking a formal education in Jewish exegesis and wisdom literature, she traveled to Israel to visit the country and her family and to research her grandmother's personal papers. This exploration culminated in Sereni's 1993 historical and biographical novel, *Il gioco dei regni* (The Game of the Kingdoms), in which the writer patiently and piercingly weaves the threads of three generations into the life of her family, entrenched in the major historical events and tragedies of the twentieth century: from the 1905 socialist Russian revolution, to zionism, fascism, nazism, the two world wars, the making of the state of Israel, Italian politics, and the culture of the twentieth century. "Much about my family is written in books: treatises, memoirs, essays, correspondence. The hero, the woman biologist, the agronomists, the nihilists, the historian, the woman secret agent, the enlightened industrialist. Some became a part of history while still living." (*Keeping House*, 54) In and out of official history, almost as though walking lightly through the house in slippers, Sereni narrates history with the discretion and, one can say, a measure of affection, that can also be found in her recipes. As ingredients in the right dosage, carefully chosen by proven experience, facts intertwine, generate, and expand like the chemical reaction that takes place in a cooking pot, threading through the inner channels of emotions, passions, beliefs, and allegiances.[10]

Sereni's writings escape clear codification. Even though, at times, she might refer to her books (with the exception of those clearly defined as essays) as novels, they don't belong to any particular genre, but are rather hybrids, composites of fact and fiction.[11] She considers herself "scrittrice di frontiera,"[12] a border writer, who ultimately avoids the dualistic distinction between fiction and nonfiction. In her works, fiction, autobiography, history, and essay blend, and women's extra-verbal codes find space—the languages of food, of home spaces, of clothing. Her narrative style has different outcomes, as it draws from various sources and motivations: personal and public, reflective and interventionist, biographical and journalistic, passionate and lucid; it is never divorced from a utopian glance, and yet remains vulnerable and transparent. The extraordinary response to the publication of *Keeping House* from women persuaded Sereni of the vital connection she established with her readers through her book. In her nonfiction writings Sereni insists on a "profound historical difference" in women's language and writing, a difference women have elaborated and developed through specific cultural experiences and competencies related to their collective and individual roles. Sereni is attracted to and interested in the variety and richness of a feminine language infused with a plurality of possible meanings and uses that can tell a story merely through gestures, smiles, and the movement of a eyebrow. "Searching for this language," Sereni remarks, "means to choose the optics of women . . . to go beyond the cultural structure overwhelmingly male oriented (and ordered), and so reach toward a gender specificity . . . that I belong to" (*Taccuino di un'ultimista*, 40, my translation).

Writing, for Sereni, is both making the self public and also carving and conquering a personal space that defines an identity both different from and in addition to a gendered one—that of a mother, for instance. The constructed self and the other thus no longer result from the oppositions of private and public, but occupy border spaces where they can move more freely and inter-dependently (Parati, 11). Her practice of "handicapped mother," expert of special needs and marginalized positions, allows her to side with the weaker individuals, experience the world from their position, and become an advocate for social changes. Her decision to accept the nomination as deputy mayor of Perugia, an educa-tional experience which she elaborates on in her last autobio-graphical novel, *Passami il sale*, was born of her desire for and conviction of the need for direct involvement in local politics. Here her poetics coincide with her praxis: "sometimes trying to put some order in the world with words is not enough for me. It seems to me that if we want to advocate real changes one cannot longer mediate nor negotiate" (*Conversazione*, 15) [my translation].

Sereni's reflections echo the sense of disillusionment and betrayal which resulted from the failed social revolution carried out by a generation of Italian leftists, so called *sessantottini* (the '68 protesters), aborted by the polarization and radicalization of the extreme left and right activists in the mid-seventies. Ironi-cally enough, between 1974 and 1976, it was a time when the electoral success of the Italian Communist Party showed the inevitability of the *compromesso storico* (historical compro-mise)—that is, the direct participation of the PCI in the Italian government as "an agent of change, order, moderation and rev-olution" in the highly suspicious and compromised hegemony of the Italian Christian Democratic Party.[13] But the extreme wings of both left and right turned terrorists brought the country to the brink of constitutional dissolution and to the terror of the infamous *anni di piombo* (years of lead), so called for the shoot-ings and killings of high profile political and business figures by both political sides. To the disappointment of the leftist activists, the Italian Communist Party did not seize the oppor-tunity to gain control and produce an ideological shift; instead it kept a low key approach and adopted a policy of national sol-idarity during the crisis. The end of the political crisis in the eighties coincided with the onset of what Sereni sees as the self-serving retreat into privacy in the eighties, a diagnosis validated in her books *Keeping House* and *Manicomio primavera*.

A brief look at Sereni's books indicates the trajectory of her generation of activist, leftist Italian intellectuals: coming of age in the late sixties and early seventies (*Sigma epsilon*), going into the retreat of the private and its examination in the eighties (*Keeping House, Manicomio primavera*); the historical revisionism of the nineties (*Il gioco dei regni*), and coming full circle, the rekindling of the abandoned revolution of the sixties, the affirmation of the will and hope to bring changes in a different society, a utopian pathos that informs her political actions and her latest books (*Eppure, Taccuino di un'ultimista, Passami il sale*).

Sereni's first book, *Sigma epsilon* (1974) is an autobiographical account of coming of age in the political activist groups in the late sixties and early seventies and an examination and critique of her generation, especially of the subaltern role of women in the still hierarchical, male-dominated power structure of the leftist political groups. Following the success of *Keeping House* in 1987, in 1989 Sereni published her first collection of short stories, *Manicomio primavera*, in which the theme of mothering handicapped children is central. None of the female protagonists of the stories retrench in denial or despair; rather they engage in a practice of life that requires the activation of new skills, as well as the ability to accept different rewards. Life for a mother of an autistic child could be an experience of maddening difficulty and understandable self-pitying. However, her sense of self-honesty, a discreet dose of utopianism toward life as a larger "project," prevails with the strategic help of femininity's gratifying clichés: a bubble bath, some make-up, a perfume or a silk dress, an elegant table at the restaurant. All are small tokens of a gendered heritage, amulets, rituals—albeit provisional and ephemeral—but indispensable to a temporary and temperate happiness.

Sereni's third book, *Il gioco dei regni*, is a biographical novel that encompasses the history and ideologies of the twentieth century through the saga of the Sereni family, who, some by choice, others by destiny, find themselves at the crossroads of major historical events: the revolutionary movements in Russia, the two world wars, Fascist jails, Nazi lagers, Stalin's totalitarism, and the zionist dream. Family members first encountered in *Keeping House* reappear in this novel in their legitimate historical and family roles. Sereni constructs the book as a montage by blending biography, autobiography, historical narrative, memoirs, and epistolary writing. In the post-face to the book, the author admits to having done a considerable amount of archival research both in Italy and in Israel, in addition to conducting countless interviews with direct sources. However, she is also interested in affirming that hers is not an historical account, but a novel, that is, invention and creation that fills empty spaces left by questions never answered. It is the writer's attempt to pick up the interactive nets that official history leaves behind, which knit together the emotional, the irrational, the ideological, such as in the passionate fervor of her Russian anarchic maternal grandmother; the Marxist Stalinism of her father; the profound sense of roots and the centrality of the family of her Jewish grandmother; the elegance and refinement of the grand aunt, all facets of a history Sereni knows too well that formed and influenced her life.

Because of the vast recycling and circularity of autobiographical material, I find it useful in my reading of Sereni's works to borrow the concept of "informed fictions," coined by Marjorie Wolf for her anthropological narratives. Wolf explains how her writings reflect her ethical and aesthetic choices, while she gives full credit to the literary construction of her documentation and researched materials. Moreover, she creates some contextually and historically plausible characters to tell and live the stories she has heard or collected from other sources. These characters also reflect and absorb the author's ethical problematic bias, personal criticism, and complicity. Sereni's autobiographical writings repropose the self and others, each time adding more pieces to the mosaics of the characters, more light and angles. These progressive and cyclical constructions of historical biographical events are well-informed fictions where fiction is understood as "narratives in which the author carefully selects and constructs the characters, events, and aspects of the self that he/she wants to make public" (Parati, 4). Whatever one writes, Sereni points out, paraphrasing Italian writer Carlo Levi, "each one of us writes always and anyway his/her own autobiography, anything he/she writes about; writing becomes the moment where experience acquires that cohesion and consequentiality that life has not, as it combines other stories, stories about others." (*Conversazione*, 19–20, my translation).

In her first successful book, *Keeping House*, Sereni weaves public and private stories around food. The relationship established between the narrator's life experiences and food generates recipes, for, as Susan J. Leonardi remarks, "Like a story, a recipe needs a recommendation, a context, a point, a reason to be" (340). Recipes are graphically separated from the narrative: the list of ingredients is followed by a very simple, first-person narration of the preparation. The reader thus is not told how to prepare a dish, as we normally see in cookbooks or on TV shows with food preparation narratives; instead we witness, or listen to the author telling us how she does it. The representational effects of Sereni's style are first of all that, the structure of the recipe, by requiring a certain conciseness, informs the language and the style of the narrative around it, producing clarity and frugal syntax. The homemade baby food opens the book in its startling simplicity: various grains are first browned then cooked in liquid to feed a difficult, crying baby. Once in a while, a touch of love, which is not included in the list of ingredients, makes its way into the text, heightening the emotional connotation of food: "at times, I add a little honey, for sweetness" (*Keeping House*, 21). Short directions are interspersed with personal reflections, advice, and brief recommendations, which are almost gestures of caring, as in this baby's vegetable soup: "I choose the greenest parts, even if hard (one must be careful with spinach because it is bitter, and cabbage because it leaves green stains even on glass). I dilute the flour in the liquid, warm it quickly and flavor it with Parmesan cheese, adding perhaps a drop of olive oil" (6). Or in the recommendation to let the bean soup "rest" a little in the bowl before eating. In establishing an active presence in her text, the narrator, in her "I" voice, welcomes her readers and the recipients of her recipes, introducing them to her own idiosyncrasies, her quirks and habits. This increasing expansion of the text of the recipe corresponds to a similar expansion of the privacy and vulnerability of the historical identity. Her recipes are the *literal* products (for we are free to copy and reproduce them) of Clara Sereni's book, which itself is a literary production.[14]

The simplicity of certain home recipes proposed in *Keeping House* indicates a preoccupation with the substance of life, with an almost ideal goodness discovered in the sixties, and revalorised once again. Unlike the first feminist wave of the sixties and seventies, here the daily repetitions, the care of children, the preparation of food and the tending of the house are not flatly refused, or passively accepted as in the pre-feminist representation; rather they become active, examined experiences. In the last chapter of *Keeping House*, devoted to the canning and preservation of food, a topic that is perfectly rendered in the Italian infinitive title "Conservare" (Preserving), the narrator, in between preserves, marmalades, and vegetables canned in oil, reflects on her relationship with her house and "homemakerness," as a means of finding and preserving her roots. The home—its habits, loneliness, and work—while allowing the woman to deepen her roots, is itself a conspicuous, expanding root demanding constant care. Sereni represents the symbiotic relation of the woman and the home as a choreography of objects and places defining and at the same time expanding the common place of homemaking: "and so my aerial self sinks into the jars, into the liqueurs, into the potted plants on the terrace, into my sweaters and blankets with which I would like to ensnare the world, into the freezer. Because in my life, pieced together with ill-fitting bits, in the mosaic of my life (as in everyone, but more so women's), keeping house can also mean a little warm place" (*Keeping House*, 142). The passage is exemplary of Sereni's extraordinary ability with her medium—language and images—as she empowers ordinary, unpoetic, domestic objects and places to unfold the woman's conflicting rapport with the home. The oxymoron "aerial roots"—a clear deterrent to the facile sublimation one may surmise from the passage—illustrates the protagonist's awareness of her unsettling condition, while the highlighted "also" ("homemaking" is *in addition* and despite its traps) conjures up a yearning in her to find in practices of homemaking comfort and stability.

The writer's full awareness that the home is a potentially risky place—self-indulgent and self-serving—can be easily inferred from her further elaboration of the "little warm place": "a small corner that is constantly changing, for its stillness would mean death, and recipes are only a base on which to build new flavors, new combinations every time" (142). *Keeping House*, as the Italian title *Casalinghitudine* more clearly suggests, is a chosen, temporary space in which to eventually carve a "little warm corner" amidst the physical and psychological existential disorder. The woman we find in this space is a literate homemaker, an intellectual with a sophisticated consciousness, engaged in examining herself and the meaning of what is "normal" as she retraces her life through dishes and meals transmitted and reinvented. The home could thus function as a gateway, a place from which to reinvent a dimension that makes it possible to overcome the limits of homemaking and of a gendered identity.

"Every cuisine tells a story," writes food writer and author Claudia Roden in *The Book of Jewish Food* (3). Worlds and generations disappear but they remain powerful in the imagination. Likewise, Roden observes, food more than anything else takes hold in people's mind with the help of all senses that capture colors, tastes, and flavors. Food that accompanies the ordinary and extraordinary occasions of life is the glue of memory. In *Keeping House* recipes acquire and accrue significance as they suture a bond with people or a life experience. There is at least one recipe for every major life event or passage, and for every significant character that takes hold of the memory and the imagination of both the narrator and reader, forming a temporary bond with the ingredients. *Pasta e fagioli* (Bean Soup) is certainly one such example for its manifesto style and its resonance in the narrator's quest for independence. Simple, humble food, a food of substance, a sloppy unappetizing meal as prepared by the father, becomes glorious comfort food in the renewed, personalized version of the emancipated protagonist. And so *Gnocchi di semolino* (Semolina Gnocchi), the dish that opens the chapter *First Courses* is the rich, carefully prepared dish of important dinners that established a partnership in the kitchen between the narrator as a child and her great aunt Ermelinda. It is the dish that carves Ermelinda into the narrator's memory as elegant, extravagant, and in charge of her upbringing. Within the dissonant memories of Ermelinda's personality—as a demanding, frivolous, and rather hard person to some—the partnership in the making of the *gnocchi* dish and her caring for the narrator's musical education and observance of Jewish rituals mark their imprint in Clara's developing identity: "For me, Aunt Mela remains a scent, music, an elegant gesture, the feeling of someone who demands much, but who is ready to give, the warmth of feeling special and unique" (40). Moreover, the scent of Aunt Mela's golden-crusted *gnocchi*, of her perfumes constitutes the "red thread" of bourgeois amenities, of love for beautiful, albeit frivolous, things and comforts that runs through the narrator's life stages.

In *Keeping House* food acts as a barometer of the shifting experience of the Italian left during the seventies and eighties, a shift due to perhaps unavoidable as well as ideological forces: rapid economic growth and rapid advance of consumerist society on the one hand, the maturation of a generation on the other hand. From collective group experience, where food is secondary and dismissed as a mere nutritional need, to the retrenching in the private, in the personal, when the young activists mature, some marry and have children and so change their relationship to food. Feverish election nights are satisfied with pizza; after-work hunger pangs with *pasta al burro* (Pasta with Butter), a dish that could be bland enough to not disturb the intense, around-the-clock work when putting out an issue of a high-flying political paper. It is not accidental that both pizza and the simple *pasta al burro* are the narrator's fast food as conformity, the group's imperatives, or the eagerness to please and be accepted take priority over quality and taste. To the narrator, who is temporarily hiding her culinary expertise and desires, viewing these almost a burden to be ashamed of, and who is in love with the editor of the paper, *pasta al burro* functions as an acceptable compromise and possible mediator:

> We had to work late, and I got to his place with a package of spaghetti, a stick of butter and a packet of grated Parmesan. We sat next to each other to eat, he even said the pasta was good (generally he never passed judgment on food, limiting himself to swallowing it to survive). For a moment it seemed that we might

open the bottle of Cordon Rouge in the refrigerator. But already his eyes were far away; he began talking about the issue of the newspaper we were preparing. (62–63)

Food is thus an indicator of the protagonist's emotional intelligence. Eventually her culinary choices cement life relationships, as in the case of her future husband. Surrounded by a circle of cinema people for whom food is mostly rarified and unsubstantial, she uses her emotional and culinary intelligence in her choice of food to prepare at a birthday party. The food, beans and hambone, is solid and simple, of peasant stock: "I wonder how I knew that it would be okay to prepare a bean dish for Massimo. Perhaps it was his frank smile, maybe his sensitive, firm hands" (94).

As food enters and operates in different social and cultural milieus, choices regarding its preparation expose class relations. One example of this is when the narrator starts to make her way in the world of her future in-laws who, unlike her own family, belong to a recently urbanized and rising middle class. In recognizing her own privileged upbringing, nurtured in taste and taught to value intangible over material things, the narrator can't conceal her annoyance at what she calls, with a perfect Italian word, *vezzi*: the acquired habits and affectations of the petit bourgeoisie. "They linger too long at the table," she remarks about her in-laws, "they eat too much, they worry too much about food. And always pasta, and sauces, and condiments, a cuisine too rich in fats and proteins . . ." (50). Sereni's reproachful tone when writing about the deterioration of healthier eating habits and foods brought about by the eagerness and rampant materialism of the emerging middle class—of former working class or southern Italian peasants—has complex ramifications. It mirrors the chasm between the educated and uneducated, and seems to anticipate the present concerns of privileged societies with unhealthy nutritional habits, especially among less affluent segments of population. In her inherently elitist position, the narrator is reclaiming for herself and for others the simplicity and goodness of fresh ingredients and humble vegetables (i.e., nettles, beans) that used to be the staples of peasant diets against the impending advance of creams and processed cheeses, which epitomize the homogenizing, apparently classless, consumerist contemporary society. A concerned and

well-directed cry, it nevertheless unveils the unmistakable paradoxi-
cal position of the Italian intellectual left, what Sereni calls the "red
bourgeoisie," and of the Italian communist cadre, a class schooled
in political thought and social commitment and raised in affluence,
privilege, and taste that has for generations lived above and beyond
the structural level.

The narrator is perfectly aware of these self-contradictions
and ironies, both as an individual and as part of a class,[15] for it is
through this recognition that she becomes deeply conscious of her
various identities. In a different moment, at a critical point, hospitalized for gestational diabetes, the goodness of a peasant dish
and of the peasant diet is refused in the name of health and self-
care. As the protagonist shares a large hospital room with several
other diabetic women, mostly from small towns in Southern Italy,
who act suspicious and derisive toward her and the signs of her
social status—her books, her diligence in keeping to the hospital
diet, the anti-stretch cream that she applies daily to her stomach—she realizes that the women disregard their strict diets in
favor of tasty and satisfying homemade foods brought to them by
their families. The other patients encourage her to eat their food
while mocking her for eating the insipid, and to them unhealth-
ful, hospital diet: "Don't worry, we'll take care of you. These
people are going to let you die" (114). The narrator's concerned
and medically disciplined attitude clashes with the seemingly irre-
sponsible and uninformed practices of the other women, with
whom she shares a serious medical condition, but from whom she
is separated by class and education.

> I didn't find it too hard to resist the temptations, except when I
> saw in front of me a container full of cabbage swimming in oil,
> the scent of onions permeating the ward. I ate my plain hospital
> vegetables courageously, feeling very brave and very stupid, amid
> a feast of cabbage and *taralli* (ring-shaped biscuits) from Puglia.
>
> And to this day I ask myself: what if I had eaten them? How
> serious would it have been? (115)

Filtered through the memory of the relentlessly self-reflective
narrator, the simple cabbage dish ironically acquires unexpected
overtones and exacerbates a personal health crisis with suspended

questions on the differently perceived relationships between food, health, and socioeconomic classes.

The representation of food as both physically and emotionally curative informs many dishes and ingredients in the book and further signifies the role of food as a metaphor for the creative exchange between memory and imagination. *Stracciatella*, a traditional, popular Roman soup made out of clear meat stock where a beaten egg is dropped and flavored with Parmesan cheese, and *Stuffed Cabbage Rolls*, an Eastern European dish, represent the foods of absence. These dishes allude to the emotional nourishment by both her father and mother that was missed in the narrator's life. The cabbage dish is the only food that evokes the narrator's mother, a connection to her Slavic origin, and an attempt to establish a point of reference to a genealogy. Because she was only few years old at the time of her mother's fatal illness and death, the narrator attempts a reconstruction of the events in a tale told in the third person. Little Clara travels with her mother and father to the USSR, the native country of her mother, where the woman is going to get treatment for her cancer. As her father becomes the only person in charge of the child, he assumes full care of her, taking the little girl with him during his meetings with the Soviet comrades and holding her in his arms in the photos. He bestows on her his undivided love and attention, attributes of a desirable, conventional father-daughter relationship that the narrator will crave thereafter and feel deprived of while growing up: a void that will be responsible for a lifelong painfully difficult and problematic relation. The care and love felt in that moment is projected and condensed in the *Stracciatella* soup that the father manages, using all his political power, to have made for his child, sick with fever, during a stop in Vienna on their way back home.

If *Stracciatella* evokes and invokes the image of an emotional, warm father, several other recipes and dishes in the book contrast that image with that of an admired but unfulfilling parent, whose rigid Stalinism eventually isolates him from the world around him. The costly and necessary struggle of the narrator to emancipate herself from being the "daughter of" and to acquire a sense of independence without loosing her roots, is central in the book, and food exemplifies the testing ground. "All my life, under my father's gaze there was an unavoidable 'but,' and each of my attempts to assert independence, freedom, take an intellectual position, would clash against his fury, or a conceited smile" (72). The young woman is competing with the suspended weight of a father who she recognizes had done better than her in "all the things I was trying to do: studying, establishing relationships, politics, even cooking" (72). The process of differentiation follows two opposite routes, that of refusal of food—a form of anorexia which at the time was diagnosed as colitis—and the more constructive and fulfilling determination to eventually leave her father's house and start nourishing herself with her own modified and invented recipes.[16]

The book closes in a self-reflective, confessional tone following the father's death, which coincides with the birth of her son. The narrator loses her roots as she plants new ones. *Amaro* (Bitter), the last recipe in the book, is not casually placed, for, as the name reveals, it is a bitter digestive drink that requires, however, one pound of sugar. Bitter and sweet at the same time, not resolved, as life itself, as exemplified by the difficult relation between daughter and father. But the last passage of *Keeping House* is actually an excerpt from a book by Sereni's father, Emilio Sereni, on the historical, nutritional evolution in Southern Italy, more specifically in the Naples area. The book ends with authoritative words about food while establishing a link to her father's favorite dish *spaghetti al pomodoro* (spaghetti with a basic tomato sauce, a dish much snubbed by the author in the book). The end is indeed emblematic, a gesture of respect for the father's contribution to the history of food and agronomy and of recognition for his contribution to her knowledge and interest in the importance and value of food. The circle seems to close, but the journey is not over. "Everything has already been said, everything has already been written" (142). Her father, his knowledge remains a base, as she hints before this quotation, from which to reinvent, recombine ingredients, reconstruct new flavors and artistic and existential strategies of regeneration to avoid extinction.

Keeping House is Sereni's intergenerational journey of self-exploration, her attempt to assemble the pieces of her life's mosaic in order to recover a past from which to build a future. Food marks rituals and seasons, continuity and changes, maturation and crises, the contradictions of a bourgeois lifestyle and the serious ideological choices. Most importantly, the life of a young woman coming of age in Italy during the sixties and seventies becomes the window for discovering and appreciating the cultural climate of a country as well as the dynamics of a family. In *Keeping House* there is a poetics of the physical order, as if in the formalization (the writing) of the recipes the narrator seeks to make sense and put some order to her life. In this process, food becomes the narrator's most instructive and creative tool to know and tell. The result is both an invitation to meditate on the various *courses* and to savor them as well.

TOASTED FLOURS

mixture of at least three types of flours

I fill a frying pan halfway with the flours and let them brown on medium heat, stirring with a wooden spatula until they brown but don't burn. The house smells of roasted nuts. I store the flour in glass jars for no more than a week, and I use it as a base for various baby meals.

MILK AND CHEESE PAPPA[1] (PORRIDGE)

I dilute flour in a little milk, rapidly warm it up on the stove, and add abundant grated Parmesan cheese.

FRUIT PAPPA

1 cup carrots
1 cup ripe fruit in season
flour to thicken

The fruit must be peeled, since these days the skin contains more pesticides than vitamins. I blend the fruit with the carrots, which have been scraped and washed. I dilute the flour in the blended mixture, and at times I add a little honey, for sweetness.

VEGETABLE PAPPA

1 cup carrots
1 cup raw greens in season

1/2 t. Parmesan cheese

flour to thicken

I choose the greenest parts, even if hard (one must be careful with spinach because it is bitter, and cabbage because it leaves green stains even on glass). I dilute the flour in the blended mixture, warm it up quickly and flavor it with Parmesan cheese, adding perhaps a drop of olive oil.

MEAT FLAVORED PAPPA

2 oz. ground horsemeat

1/2 t. Parmesan cheese

I cook the meat in a double boiler for half an hour and then squeeze it. For the baby I only use the juice (the meat can be utilized for a meat loaf). I stir the flour into the meat juice, let it cool, and flavor with Parmesan cheese.

Tommaso cried all the time. His clinical chart read: "mournful cry." Back home from the hospital, he still cried. My experienced girlfriends would tell me: "You'll see, for the first forty days they all do that, and then they settle down." Forty days went by, and my girlfriends said: "You'll see, with the first solid foods . . ."

We didn't have any money. The baby received presents of beautiful little clothes, but more savvy friends quietly brought us a box or two of powdered milk. I went back to work in desperation, dissatisfied even with the things that used to give me pleasure. My friends who were looking for their first job said: "It's better for you this way, otherwise you will become too attached to the baby." Massimo was doing the mothering, not by choice, and I would come home from work weighted down with anxieties and diapers.

The time for the first solid foods came: jars of baby food, vegetable broth, enriched pasta, but Tommaso kept on crying: large bottles of chamomile and linden tea would appease him for a few minutes, then he would start crying again, and would not sleep. He would quiet down during his bath (with the acrobatics of handling heating units, warm bath towels, checking the water temperature with my elbow after the thermometer broke), but once out of the water he would start crying again.

The pediatrician, schooled in Catholicism, diagnosed colic and blamed us for making him eat too much. He suggested that Tommaso's greedy anxiety was a sort of vice to be eradicated as soon as possible with a strict diet, without indulging in pointless compassion so full of risks for the future. For the entire length of the examination Tommaso was screaming and kicking; when I put his clothes back on, he was covered with red patches down to his navel. I was sweating and exhausted.

My experienced friends began to suggest antihistamines, others advised letting him cry "so he would not become spoiled." Everybody talked about the whims of children, little monsters always ready to take advantage of us. We began to feel isolated, taking turns staying up with Tommaso and almost ashamed to admit it: their criticism of over-protectiveness did not help our nights, devastated by too much coffee and by his desperate crying.

By his fourth month, Tommaso had lots of curls and a single white hair, but his very deep blue eyes were always swollen, and he wore a furious expression; he was hardly sleeping at all. At best he slept half an hour, only after hours and hours of rocking and lullabies. Dissent around us was growing.

Part of my capacity to survive depends on the fact that I can count on two or three gods of the hearth, each with its own sphere of action: they don't cast judgments, and in crucial moments they provide guidance and set up action. I can trust them, I can even follow their advice. I still give daily mental thanks to the deity that suggested seeing a homeopathic physician, a solution that until that moment had eluded me.

We faced the prospect with a certain resignation: we had already seen so many doctors, and Tommaso had cried desperately with each white coat.

The homeopath was wearing house slippers and a corduroy jacket. He played with Tommaso, made him laugh, stretched him and checked him without complaints on his part. He proclaimed that the baby was starving; hunger was tugging at his stomach and his heart, he said.

Perplexed, we left the doctor's office with a recipe for toasted, whole wheat flour, a number of fruit and vegetable shakes, and horsemeat. Had we not been so desperate we probably wouldn't have tried this.

In the course of three or four days Tommaso began to be placated; there was no longer need for acrobatic maneuverings of bottle and pacifier to make sure he wouldn't choke on the milk, and he was even sleeping a little longer. A part of his emptiness was filled up.

But he did not stop crying at night with the sorrowful, terrible cry of a child who seemed to have lost something.

2

appetizers

ARUGULA SPREAD

1/2 cup ricotta
1 bunch of arugula
2 T. oil
pinch of salt
whole wheat bread

I chop the arugula coarsely and mix it with the ricotta, oil, and salt. I let it stand for at least twelve hours and then spread it thickly on slices of whole wheat bread.

ANCHOVY SANDWICHES

panini (small, crusty rolls)
fresh mozzarella
butter
anchovy paste

I split the rolls in half, removing some of the soft part of the bread from the middle of each half, and spread butter on each. I place slices of mozzarella on top of the two halves, followed by a layer of anchovy paste.

Immediately before bringing them to the table, I put the sandwiches in a hot oven for a few minutes. When I have the time and inclination, I secure the two halves of each roll with a toothpick to keep them from coming apart or losing their shape.

SALAMI SPREAD

Hungarian salami
full-flavored green olives
butter
sliced bread, cut into 4 smaller squares

I chop part of the salami finely and mix it with an equal amount of butter, stirring for a while with a wooden spoon in order to obtain a soft and fluffy mixture.

I then spread a thin layer of it on the bread slices and top with a slice of salami and half a pitted olive.

BREAD AND MORTADELLA

stracchino cheese (a soft, creamy cheese)
mortadella
olive oil
bread rolls

I split the rolls and cover both halves with a generous layer of cheese. On the top I place a very thin slice of mortadella.

SAVORY CROSTINI

2 loaves of stale French bread
1/2 cup butter
I T. flour
1/2 cup broth
1 small tube of anchovy paste
2 T. salted capers
2 T. chopped parsley

I melt the butter in a small saucepan, add the flour and cook it for a minute or two, stirring well, then I add the broth. I keep stirring until the sauce, which of course must be smooth and free of lumps, thickens. I then add the anchovy paste, the capers, which I have rinsed and chopped, the parsley, and sometimes (but I would say almost never) a bit of salt. The mixture is then spread on thin slices of stale bread, dotted with butter, and placed for a few minutes in a warm oven.

Grandmother Alfonsa, who had never been a peasant by any means, and who had never visited a country village except in search of a wet-nurse, used to dress in black like a peasant woman, in shapeless, multi-layered dresses that reached nearly to the ground. She had big feet, wore men's socks, and black, laced shoes just like my father's. She looked like the ugly sister of her two other very beautiful sisters (Aunt Elena and Aunt Ermelinda), and she did everything to appear even more awkward, graceless, inelegant. As she aged, she came to resemble Golda Meir. When she was young, she was rather pretty, but the two or three photos of her as a young woman were not in the family album: nobody ever looked at them, nor did she seem to want to remember them.

Aunt Ermelinda had been a lady-in-waiting at the royal court of Italy and Aunt Elena had mingled in high society, displaying magnificent clothes and jewels. Grandmother Alfonsa had channeled her life's energies into being courageous, facing her children's choices, and accepting their deaths.

She must not have complained much during her life: all her grief and pain seemed to have thickened in the lines of her face and in her gestures, which were stiff and hardened. She frightened me; there were no acceptable excuses with her.

I saw her only sporadically, as she lived in Israel, at that time called Palestine. The worst thing my father could threaten me with was, "I am going to write about this to *mammà*." That must be why I have such a dark memory of a person everyone else unconditionally adored.

In Israel, Grandmother Alfonsa raised chickens and gave constant proof of her courage and energy: the years had curved her nose into an anti-semitic caricature. When in Italy—she was usually called in during family emergencies—she managed our complicated household efficiently, cutting everything superfluous without hesitation, in obstinate opposition to Aunt Ermelinda's systematic frivolity. It was understood between the two of them that I would not be made to feel deprived. Meanwhile, she made me gulp down medicine without much fuss and made sure that my red and white checked smocks were clean and ready. But the buttons she sewed back on were always mismatched and hastily put on with little regard for esthetics.

The golden rule in the kitchen was very simple: "you eat what is put on the table," which in my father's political realism translated as *o ti mangi questa minestra o ti butti dalla finestra* ("either you eat this soup or you jump out of the window"). Never very hungry, I would gloomily take my seat at the table. Seeing me hesitate as I chewed, unable to swallow my food, my father would launch into a children's story along the lines of mischievous Peter Porcupine, adding embellishments such as mice in the soup. Fortunately, the food was generally simple and without flights of fancy; not even kosher cuisine was represented among Grandmother's dishes, which were chosen mostly on the basis of nutritional value and low cost. As far as I can remember, only once did she venture to prepare a sweet and sour meat dish: the revolt of the entire family was particularly unanimous, and after eating the leftovers herself for several meals, she finally had to agree to get rid of what was left.

Wartime hunger was still a reality, and nothing was thrown away. Whether it was her family background (she was one of fourteen brothers and sisters) or her atavistically thrifty Jewish stock, Grandmother Alfonsa was capable of recycling everything: leftover stew went into meatballs, pieces of dry cod into fritters.

When I was growing up in the fifties and store bought cookies were unaffordable, a much appreciated snack were slices of dry bread (eaten without butter, because I had acetonemia), kept in a large, red tin box. When I started to make *crostini* in my own home, for a while I used fresh bread instead of stale bread, a conscious act of waste in order for me to cut the umbilical cord.

BASIL SPREAD

> 1/4 cup ricotta
> 2 T. basil
> 1 T. oil
> salt
> olive bread

I chop the basil and add it to the ricotta with the oil and salt and mix all in the blender (this is recent; I used to use a sieve). I set the mixture aside for at least half a day, then spread it generously on thin slices of bread about 1/2 inch thick.

TUNA SPREAD

1 cup ricotta
1/2 cup tuna in oil
1 hard-boiled egg
juice of one lemon
whole wheat bread

I mix all ingredients well and try to whip them a bit with a mixer. I then spread the mixture on thin slices of whole wheat bread.

EGGPLANT PANINI

sliced fried eggplant
mozzarella
tomato paste
or
leftover eggplant Parmesan
soft rolls

I cut the rolls lengthwise, remove some of the soft part from the middle replacing it with eggplant, mozzarella, and a dab of tomato paste. Five minutes before bringing them to the table, I warm them up briefly in a hot oven.

Around the mid-seventies, when Massimo and I felt that we wanted to build a solid relationship, he introduced me to the "group." I was admitted as a sort of apprentice, whose full acceptance would eventually have to be decided.

The monolithic group, apparently void of edges or contradictions, appeared to me as a fortress to conquer, and there was no doubt that it was paramount for Massimo that I succeed in the quest. Therefore, I tried obstinately to adapt to the group, making myself always available, more so than I cared to.

My capacity to recycle leftovers and scraps was put to the test several times by the sudden, merry pangs of hunger that would overtake us late at night, in the middle of a heated political discussion. Score a point for me, I thought, as I invented a supper.

The first time that I was invited over, I had bad wine, stale bread, and carelessly cooked sausage. I began to have my first doubts.

PANINI WITH BEANS

stewed beans
homemade bread

I spread a layer of leftover beans between two slices of homemade bread and put it under the broiler for a few minutes. Better still if I have at hand a grill with hot coals.

CELERY WITH GORGONZOLA

1 bunch celery
1/2 cup of Gorgonzola
1/3 cup of mascarpone cheese
1 T. whiskey
2 T. grated Parmesan cheese

I clean the celery well, removing all hard strings and choosing the whitest stalks. In the celery cavity, using a knife, I spread the paste that I have obtained by thoroughly blending the two cheeses and the whiskey.

FRIED BREAD (CROUTONS)

When I prepare sandwiches, I save the unused parts, such as the soft part of the rolls, the crust of sliced bread, and the various useless pieces to make fried bread, which can be eaten as it is or added to pureed vegetables or to eggs for Bocconcini Omelette.

MARINATED ZUCCHINI

zucchini
salt
vinegar
parsley

I cut the zucchini lengthwise into 1/2 inch slices and fry them in hot boiling oil. After drying them thoroughly on brown paper (or paper towels), I place them in a container with a lid. On the top of the layered and salted zucchini I pour a little warm vinegar, flavored with parsley.

They need to rest in a cool place for at least ten hours, but they will keep for much longer than that.

BRAISED TOMATOES

For each tomato:
half of a boiled potato
2 T. tuna in oil
1 t. salted capers
half of a hard-boiled egg
1 T. of mayonnaise, and more mayonnaise for topping

After removing the tops of red, firm round tomatoes, I extract the pulp and salt the inside. I let them drain upside down for an hour. I mix all other ingredients together except for the egg, and fill the tomatoes with the mixture. Finally, I top each tomato with the hard-boiled egg, yolk side down, and a swirl of mayonnaise all around.

The script of the first six years of my life is a seamless melodrama. Precocious and sensitive, I was the little orphan with the big sad eyes, wearing smocked piqué dresses, walking through rooms and halls inhabited by books, old people, ghosts.

Having lost my mother at a very tender age, by right I deserved a good dose of sympathy: teachers and neighbors had love and tenderness for me as they exchanged meaningful looks.

Equally melodramatic was my father's relationship with a much younger woman: above my head fluttered words such as "relationship" and "stepmother."

On the way back from City Hall in Rome's Capitol Hill, as I sat between my father and his new bride in a black and gray suit, holding a bouquet of violets, I asked if I could call her mommy. That afternoon there was a reception at our house (Aunt Ermelinda in high fashion, and Grandmother Alfonsa already prepared to leave), after which my father set off for the Senate House to discuss the so-called Swindle Law.[1]

Sympathy became ambiguous and malignant, and the story-line was becoming tangled: instead of being dressed in rags and ashes, instead of being beaten and pushed in the corner as in Grimm's fairytales (my father with a rare sense of timing had given me the complete collection of them just at that time), my stepmother was weaving with me an alliance made of dolls' dresses and our shared lack of appetite. I never got dirty, I was not greedy, didn't break toys, never got bruises or scratches, and I never lost the buttons on my dresses. Alarmed, she immediately taught me how to play jump rope and hopscotch.

For a while after the wedding, my father emerged more often from the entrenchment of his study, where an enormous portrait of Stalin in the socialist realist style stood watch above the door. The contradiction between taste/culture and politics must not have played an insignificant part in my father's life. When we moved into another house in the last months of 1956, the portrait ended up in the cellar without any outcry. And for a while, during my playtime, I would go and see it, drawn to this figure with the moustache and benevolently paternal air. Later, the oil-based color became moldy, or maybe I became older and other father figures appeared on my horizon.

"Mommy" was shaking off the aftermath of a serious illness, therefore it was permitted to indulge her and spoil her a little. Her lack of interest in food loosened the discreet but firm hold Grandmother Alfonsa still kept on the household. In order to tickle her own appetite and show that she was the lady of the house, Mommy served braised tomatoes and creativity, and for me she reserved tender lettuce hearts and other delicacies.

Grandmother Alfonsa returned to Palestine. Aunt Ermelinda kept her place at the head of the table, but I no longer sat next to her: with the typical cynicism of children, having to choose between the older woman and the younger one, I did not hesitate.

CROSTINI WITH LIVER

12 oz. chicken livers and other giblets
1 small onion
1 handful of salted capers, well rinsed

4 juniper berries
1 T. flour
1 T. tomato paste
1 T. anchovy paste
1/4 cup wine
1/4 cup vinegar
oil
salt
homemade bread

I brown a finely chopped onion with the liver in the oil. After ten minutes, I add the capers and the juniper berries and cook for another minute or two, then remove from the heat and pass it through a sieve with large holes in order to obtain a rather grainy purée. I return the purée to the skillet, add the flour, wine, vinegar, anchovy paste, tomato paste, and later a little water or broth and let it cook for another fifteen minutes.

It should be spread while very hot on slices of homemade bread. In Cetona they were first dipped in broth, but I prefer them oven crisp.

When the two couples, Massimo and I and Lucio and Marta, chose to vacation together in Cetona, the cast-iron unity of the group was challenged, something that had never been done openly.

At the time, Marta and Lucio were on the fringe of what constituted the "hard core" of the group: this, as well as their self-indulgence for beautiful things, comforts, pleasures, drew them closer to me.

The heart of the group was Aldo. The unrest of the Trento experience was over, but it was in Trento that Aldo had learned how to do politics as well as other things.[2] He learned that workers looked with suspicion at parkas, and so he sported a little gray overcoat, while his slacks, a bit too short, showed his overwashed socks with their loosened elastic. He also learned that Sit-Siemens' workers ate large quantities of overcooked and badly seasoned pasta, which now placated some of his anxieties and hunger, and that the oppressive grayness of the factory could be broken by flowers on the windows of the Porto Marghera workers' dorms.

He religiously grew a red, healthy geranium, the only colorful note in his otherwise austere and faded house. He made sharp judgments about everybody, himself included, driven by his desire for an abstract yet deeply felt sense of morality. Incapable of living in a gray area, he wavered between a noncritical enthusiasm for my sense of autonomy and a barely concealed disdain for my grandmother's silver samovar.

The others in the group adapted differently to his dictates with varying levels of discomfort.

In Cetona we rented a small house because I feared invasions by both the group and Massimo's family.

Marta was beautiful, elegant, full of vitality. Next to her Lucio looked like a bloodless wren whose power inside their relationship came to him from his political past (he had been a national party executive and Marta a little "red guard") and from a rigorous, militant culture. Marta was hesitant and unsure, her voice acquiring definition only when she was talking about her work as a teacher. Like many relationships, theirs was not an easy one.

We spent three weeks sleeping like logs, playing cards, reading, exploring the surrounding area, and experimenting in the kitchen. In the nearby Belvedere restaurant, among Disneyland-style reproductions of prehistoric monsters, trees, and animals, we had discovered Tuscan *crostini*, whose taste we tried to reproduce several times by adjusting the seasoning a little here and a little there.

Toward the end of the vacation we felt just a little bored, and we had reached an almost perfect harmony among the four of us. In the kitchen, whose exterior wall was covered with caper bushes, the crock was steaming, full of creamed chicken livers. It was raining and we had already gone on many excursions, so the plan for the day was to eat as many crostini as we wanted, accompanied by a bottle of good wine, already open: red wine of course, to warm up a precocious autumn. Framed by the window overlooking the valley below, the rain, like a curtain, shaded the gentle lines of the Tuscan hills. Being inside gave us a feeling of laziness and well-being.

Under the pouring rain a figure stood still on the street corner, hesitant and alarming, his arms dripping along his sides.

We heard the door bell. In the doorway stood Aldo, drenched and shivering: we couldn't help but love him and make room for him among us.

With the first flash of his eyes, the affection of the first hug quickly disappeared. He dried his hair and was already aggressive. Massimo and Lucio immediately tuned to the latest political events, Marta and I kept stirring and protecting our cooking pot.

We sat down at the table. Still talking, he said he was not hungry and dismissed with poisonous irony the brand of our good wine. His refusal was weighing on us, as if we were wasting time. We didn't eat much either, sucked in by his logic, feeling already ashamed of our little home in the village compared to his tent pitched among the rocks and vipers of the mountain.

The nearly full pot sat at the center of the table. We were discussing politics when we should have been talking about ourselves.

Absentmindedly, Aldo took a slice of bread and with a knife covered it with the liver pâté, and proceeded to eat an enormous quantity of it.

SEMOLINA GNOCCHI

1 qt. milk
10 oz. semolina flour
3 egg yolks
2 oz. grated Parmesan cheese
2 oz. butter
salt

I heat the milk with the salt; when it is boiling I sprinkle in the semolina. When the semolina is more or less cooked (after about ten minutes), I remove the pot from the burner and add the other ingredients, mixing thoroughly and quickly, so that the eggs don't cook. I then pour the mixture on a marble table surface, and smooth it out to a thickness of half a centimeter at most, using the wet blade of a knife. I let the mixture cool completely, and cut it into squares, or into circles by using a demitasse. I arrange the pieces in two or three layers in a greased baking dish, which I put into a hot oven (480° F.) for fifteen minutes or until golden brown. Naturally, I serve the gnocchi in the baking dish.

Elementary school teacher, ex-lady-in-waiting to the queen, pianist, puzzle fanatic, polyglot, a childless widow with beautiful white hair in an old-fashioned hairdo, and with an ailing leg that allowed her to show off her magnificent walking sticks, Aunt Ermelinda lived in the apartment next door. She ate her meals with us, always on the alert to check how I held my silverware, and whether I was sitting up straight.

I called her Aunt Mela (Aunt Apple) because of her cheeks, taut and fresh despite her eighty years: stroking them was a pleasure of which I keep an exact memory, like her scent, made up of cologne, Marseille soap, and years carried with pride.

For every generation, Aunt Mela had chosen for herself a favorite child to raise with every care and to turn into—if possible—a genius. The generation of my father, his brothers, his cousins, was certainly the most fruitful in this sense; subsequently, the flame of genius gradually grew weaker with the war, the racial laws, emigration, with a life that was too different from that for which she was prepared. She did not appear troubled: she voted socialist and embroidered pillows for benefit fairs in the Jewish community. Even the absence of males to entrust with the family's Italian destiny did not appear to worry her: she chose me, taking on the task of passing on to me all the knowledge likely to make me a person of genius.

They say that when I was little I had a tin ear. Aunt Ermelinda sat me in front of the piano when I was three: she blocked the swivel stool that might have been a source of danger or distraction, and set about making me practice, day after day, in the worst hours of the afternoon, when all the other children in the building played in the courtyard: scales, exercises, solfeggios, Burgmuller, Clementi, and then Beethoven.

Upon returning from his trips, my father came to hear me play. He would sit on the velvet sofa with an air of concentration, to see whether or not I had made progress.

When my mother died I was allowed a respite (a relief that I could not show), then the piano lessons—which included being forced to listen to Aunt Ermelinda's virtuosity—began again, with pieces of unleavened bread as a prize and snack. It was in strips, to be broken off one by one so that it would last longer. On special occasions, when I had played very well and without too much coaxing, some fruit-flavored candies were produced from a silver box that must have been an incense holder.

I searched for pardons and, if possible, absolutions. One afternoon I made myself cry over Chopin's Funeral March that Aunt Mela was hammering out on the piano, almost on top of it; she looked like the mad pianist in the film *Piccoli di Podrecca*

(The Children of Podrecca) that she herself had taken me to see. I stretched out dramatically on the sofa, my face pressed into the darkness of my arms as though I were crying: I really wanted to think about my mother buried in Lausanne, but I was searching for an image that was already escaping me. Aunt Ermelinda noticed me only after she had gone on to a piece from *La Traviata*, and reproached me because she thought I had fallen asleep.

She was going to make a genius out of me, so she allowed me to participate in her beauty regimen, so I would hand her hairpins and clips, and occasionally she would let me stroke the old silk of the kimonos of her youth. I would touch her elegance made of sables, silver foxes, unpolished pearls, and ruby brooches. She would let me glimpse into her past, immortalized on glass plates to be inserted into a strange apparatus something like a wooden view-master, regal and delicate, or documented in her old dance cards from the royal palace balls. I would take a look at our roots, inscribed in the family tree hanging beside her bed. Many rituals, each with its own function.

My father had left the Jewish community, but Aunt Ermelinda was a practicing Jew. If there were ever disagreements in this area, I was never made to suffer for it: a Purim dress, Jewish songs, the story of the Maccabees, of past heroes and ancient rabbinical glories were all allowed to enter my life without dispute. The world of religion appeared exotic and wonderful to me, without giving me a particular desire to enter it.

At night, in the dark (nightlights were considered an indulgence for the weak, the only light to cling to was the one coming through the keyhole), to be on the safe side I recited the Catholic prayers I learned in school. In their essays, my schoolmates described their first communion as the most beautiful day of their lives; I compared it with my own witnessing of the civil wedding between my father and stepmother. *Épater les bourgeois* was a recurrent phrase in our family vocabulary, surprising people was the only weapon with which I felt some control.

In middle school, when the diversity of being atheist weighed on me, I professed Judaism.

When Tommaso was born, and a new interpretation of the world began for me, the fact that my son had a surname that was not Jewish made me feel safe from certain dangers. But there was so much ancestral pride in hearing him go around the house singing ". . . one and only creator *barush, barushemà*. . . ."

For Yom Kippur, Aunt Ermelinda, who almost never cooked, prepared an excellent dinner. There had to be several delicacies, but it was the olives that held the greatest fascination for me: black, very big, completely different from the little sickly ones that I ate in Formia. Seated at the head of the table in her most elegant dress, Aunt Ermelinda proceeded to surround herself with big plates, little plates, glasses, and silverware in great quantities; our normal dinner was brightened by her rituals, and there were always a few olives set aside for me.

In the domestic chaos that preceded the important dinners that required her supervision, Aunt Ermelinda firmly carved out a space for her semolina gnocchi. We went off to prepare them in her own kitchen, just the two of us, while our apartment bustled with preparations. She buttered the baking dish and cut out the circles with an almost religious devotion. The gold of their crust was a guarantee that not even among important guests, not even in the midst of the most heated discussions in incomprehensible languages, would she forget to check whether I was sitting properly, or adjust my hair clip.

Family memories pass on an image of Ermelinda Pontecorvo-Sereni as a woman who was hard, stingy, despotic, all in all not very pleasant. Unbearably frivolous, she had not given up her extravagant jewelry even during the war (she wore it so naturally; its value depended on its history and not on its price. It was stolen from her, and soon afterwards she died, uprooted, without so much as a sapphire to pin her shawl closed). For me, Aunt Mela remains a scent, music, an elegant gesture, the feeling of someone who demands much, but who is ready to give, the warmth of feeling special and unique.

CHESTNUT GNOCCHI

4 oz. white flour
4 oz. chestnut flour
salt

I knead the ingredients with just enough water, forming thin logs that I then cut into small 1/2-inch sections. I cook them in plenty of salted water, drain them, and dress with a walnut sauce (a handful of finely chopped walnuts warmed together with light cream and a little Parmesan).

HAM GNOCCHI

2 oz. boiled ham
2 egg yolks
Parmesan cheese
potato gnocchi

I cook the gnocchi as usual. Meanwhile I chop the ham finely and mix it in with the egg yolks. I drain the gnocchi and pour the sauce over them, mixing thoroughly and adding a little Parmesan.

GNOCCHI WITH COGNAC

8 oz. Gorgonzola with mascarpone cheese
3 T. cognac
potato gnocchi

I dissolve the Gorgonzola with the steam and a little of the cooking water from the gnocchi, which must be well drained. I dress them with the melted cheese, and add the cognac at the last minute.

PASTA E FAGIOLI (PASTA WITH BEANS)

2 cans pinto beans
2 oz. bacon
1 medium onion
1 t. tomato paste
1 1/2 cups water
6 oz. spaghetti, broken up

I sauté the chopped onion and bacon. When the onion becomes golden I add the beans along with their liquid, the tomato paste, a pinch of salt. I let it simmer for about ten minutes, I add the water and bring it to a boil. Add the pasta, and let it boil on a high flame for two or three minutes. At this point, I remove it from the stove, and allow it to finish cooking in the hot pan.

It was summertime, time for separations and absences. My ear ached, and so did my soul: probably the man I was in love with and on whom I blamed all my unhappiness (a gesture I sometimes acknowledge as unfair), the man of a thousand commitments had cancelled a date with me. Maybe it was for dinner together—first the cafeteria, then his overflowing ashtrays, and my unvoiced desire to uncork a certain bottle of Cordon Rouge, the only occupant of my deserted refrigerator.

I cradled my ear in my pillow, a little dazed, my head throbbing.

Enrico came over; he was my best friend. He was there when I had a fever, when robbers broke down my door, and when it looked like I might be going to England for an abortion.

Enrico sat next to me on the big brass bed that squeaked at every movement while my ear rested on the pillow. As the pain in my soul diminished, it was gradually replaced, first by a light appetite, then by hunger.

"I feel like *pasta e fagioli*," I said, "But just like they make it in the country, with the beans dissolving into a thick soup, cold, with broken-up spaghetti in it. . . ."

That dream of *pasta e fagioli* began to dance before our eyes almost tangibly. We tried to think where we might be able to eat such a dish, but we couldn't think of any place—restaurant or *trattoria*, in Rome or outside—that would guarantee fulfillment of our fantasy.

With Enrico I could take risks—with everything but love—and so I gave it a try.

The only bean soup that I had ever seen being made was the one my father liked: cannellini beans boiled in water with a garlic clove and a little oil, the rice cooked separately and added at the end. I detested it with good reason, I think. So I consulted Enrico, who had more wholesome family traditions. I relied in part on my culinary instinct and, above all, I made do with what I had in the house.

The smell of the sauté permeated the rooms, the dream was taking form. Then we had to wait for the beans to start breaking apart before putting in the pasta, which was still very *al dente* when we put the soup in the bowls to let it rest.

This was the most difficult moment because I hadn't even eaten lunch, and because trying to make a dream come true is always dangerous.

We were seated face to face at the light blue table, with the beans in the center—delicious—feeling our togetherness and the assurance of that distant complicity we had always shared.

What revenge on my father's white beans, and on my brother-in-law, who had warned me when I left home: "Go ahead, go live by yourself: you don't know what it means to live on *pasta e fagioli*."

Beans became my banner; I have prepared them for dinners, suppers, picnics, boasting about their protein contents and the healthful nutrition of the pioneers of the American west.

Time has made me more thrifty, Tommaso and health fads have made me more careful about nutrition: from canned beans I have moved on to use dried beans, soaked the day before; organizing and planning ahead are more important now than improvising.

The far west—fascination and fear, risk and adventure—is really far away now.

SEVEN GRAIN SOUP

4 medium onions
1 handful each of:
red beans
black beans
lentils
garbanzos
soy beans
wheat
pearl barley
spelt
18 oz. mixed vegetables for minestrone
1 T. tomato paste
oil
salt

I coarsely chop the onions and cook them in oil until golden.
I add the grains, previously soaked in water for twelve hours (the
spelt and pearl barley are the most tender, it's enough to put them
in water for about ten minutes), the tomato paste, the salt, and
enough water to cover. I cook it almost completely (for an hour if
it is in a pressure cooker), then I add the vegetables. Sometimes I
partially puree it with a hand-held mixer, so that the individual
components break up, but not completely.

If one envisions a Jewish turn-of-the-century doctor, presented
at Court, one cannot help imagining him as keen-eyed, with a
goatee, a dignified stance. Grandfather Nello was exactly like
this, all in a compact size; in fact, the king of Italy—who, it was
well known, had lowered the minimum height requirements for
the military service—was happy to have him at his side in official
photos, in order to show off his own extra inches of height.

In family history, this Samuele is a wan figure, immortalized by
innumerable photos. The only merit unanimously given him,
besides his few one-liners, was his having enlightened an entire generation of mothers to the most advanced standards of child-rearing.

When Tommaso was a few months old and was eating his
whole grain cereals, one of those mothers told me about Seven
Grain Soup. Grandfather Nello firmly insisted that children be
given soups with a variety of legumes and cereals, in order that
their properties could complement each other.

Much more can be said on the subject of Seven Grain Soup
and its regional variations and names: *Panspermía* is a popular
good-luck ritual, in its various epochs and forms, among all peo-
ples, the Genoese *mess-ciùa* derives from the right given to dock
workers to gather up the grains leaked out of the sacks that were
being loaded. In my mother-in-law's town, a bowl of mixed cereal
called *i vertuti* (the virtues) was prepared for the feast of the
Madonna, the fifteenth of August, and offered to all the children.

Tommaso grew, and after all the baby cereals, we graduated
to the nursery school on Forlí Street. I say *we* because it was a
strange school; an island of 1968 that had struggled to survive. It
required an unusual amount of participation on the part of the
parents, an involvement that was at times onerous. There was nei-

ther cook nor kitchen; faced with the prospect of children sent to school with lunchboxes, we arranged instead to take turns cooking a complete meal for forty children.

The first year my desire for recognition was bitterly frustrated: for all the effort I put into it, the children were finicky, I was a beginner, and the pressure cookers that I used to transport the food came back almost full, along with disapproving looks from the teachers, heavy feelings of guilt, and Tommaso who could not boast about his mother.

I had been told that children did not like soup, but it was the thing I knew best, and with which I felt most confident.

I was feeling a little less sure, however, when I arrived at the school with the pots, and the teacher who opened them said:

"Soup," raising her eyebrows.

She tasted, paused, and smiled: the first door had been opened, and she announced a delicious soup.

The children had seconds; Lisetta put the bowl on her head hat-like to show her appreciation. But Tommaso refused to take part in my success.

NETTLE SOUP

1 bunch nettles
1/2 chicken breast
1 qt. stock
8 T. semolina

I use only the young, tender leaves of the nettles, gathered in the spring, carefully washed in cold water (it goes without saying that gloves are a must). I toss them into the boiling stock, together with the chicken breast, finely diced. After about ten minutes, I sprinkle in the semolina and stir while cooking.

PUMPKIN SOUP

2 lbs. pumpkin, peeled and thinly sliced
2 cups stock
2 oz. butter
2 T. flour

croutons
Parmesan cheese

I cook the pumpkin in the stock, then I pass it through a sieve.
I add the flour to the butter melted in a pan, and when it is golden
I add the stock and pureed pumpkin. To be eaten very hot, with
croutons and a little Parmesan.

CREAM OF PEAS

1 large onion
2 oz. prosciutto (including the fat), finely chopped
18 oz. shelled peas
2 t. grated Parmesan
oil
salt

I chop the onion and sauté it in the oil until golden, along
with the prosciutto. I add the peas and salt. I cook for three or
four minutes stirring, then I add two cups of warm water and finish cooking on low heat. I obtain a rather thick soup that I then
put in the blender or food mill. The Parmesan cheese is optional.

A few months passed without my father and me seeing each
other. When I had to go home to get clothes and books, my mother
made tea for me and the friend whom I brought with me (I was
not sure that everything would proceed without a snag, so for pro-
tection and possible flight I did not go alone), while he remained
shut in his room "resting," even though it was six in the evening.
Our first meeting took place on neutral ground, or so it
should have been in theory, but the meeting at the front door of
Via delle Botteghe Oscure[1] forced us into a formal show of affection because of the many witnesses that we somehow had to keep
in mind.
He took me to lunch in a fancy restaurant nearby: dim light-
ing, prized paintings, impeccable service, a hushed, luxurious
atmosphere.
At home I had always heard lectures about there never being
enough money: if our living quarters betrayed a financial status

foreign to my classmates, my clothing however was always the most makeshift, handed down, and the least fashionable of any of my peers. Of the living quarters I was not aware, of the rest I was, and it bothered me, even though I could not even imagine questioning the militant intellectual and political choices that appeared to determine this situation.

That lunch was a revelation about my relationship with my father, not only for the terrible things he was saying to me, but also about his relationship with the outside world, for the poise with which he moved about the high-class restaurant, for the haughtiness that he showed in the selection of wine (at home we didn't drink any), for the ease with which he paid the bill.

So it was possible that he had a sort of a double life: the great, scintillating speaker whose myth was beginning to reach my ears, the Teacher capable of passing culture on to generations of students. At home, with me, culture was like an act of terrorism, politics remained anecdotal, never becoming dialogue or exchange of ideas. The critical gourmet, who at home imposed monotonous diets and insipid foods.

I was in the midst of these confused reflections as I flooded first my pea soup, then my veal breast, with tears of frustration. I didn't eat, but I gave myself the satisfaction of smoking in front of him for the first time.

The pea soup came to my mind again many times, either from actual hunger or from a desire for the luxurious, the superfluous, the beautiful.

I hadn't even tasted it, so I couldn't reconstruct its flavor; I recreated it a year later, as soon as I had a home and a stove.

CREAM OF LETTUCE

1 lb. lettuce
2 oz. butter
2 T. flour
2 cups milk
2 cups stock
1 egg yolk
2 T. grated Parmesan cheese

I bring the milk and stock to a boil, and cook the lettuce in it, removing it when it is still *al dente*. After draining it, I pass it through a sieve. In a pan I melt the butter, add the flour, and when they are well mixed, I add the creamed lettuce and the cooking liquid. I let it cook for fifteen minutes, then I pour it in a soup tureen in which I have already beaten the egg yolk and Parmesan.

ZUCCHINI SOUP

1 lb. zucchini
1 lb. onions
1 lb. San Marzano tomatoes[2]
1 egg
2 T. Parmesan cheese
2 T. Romano cheese
oil
salt
homemade bread

I cook the sliced onions, the tomatoes sliced into quarters, and the zucchini (cut into large matchsticks) in the oil over high heat for about twenty minutes. When the vegetables are cooked but not overdone, I add two cups of water and the salt. I bring the mixture to a boil for two or three minutes, then add the egg yolk beaten with the Parmesan and Romano cheeses. I then pour the piping hot soup over slices of homemade bread, preferably toasted.

Of Massimo's mother I knew the courteous telephone manners, of his father I had heard occasional stories about his unsophisticated bursts of anger, mingled with infantile destructiveness. At Christmastime Massimo had surprised me with an enormous slice of the cassata[3] that concluded the family dinner: the initiative was not his, but his mother's. But after all, I had helped him wrap his gifts, and my crepe paper folded into a flower or candy wrapper shape had made a mark in their routine. I had no particular desire or interest in becoming closer to them, but at a certain point it became necessary. There came an invitation to dinner: their embarrassment and mine, the house sparkling, plates and glasses carefully lined up, the silver not set according to etiquette. Egg noodles, sauces, heavy cream, peas and mushrooms, much meat, many side dishes. I observed dispassionately, unconsciously bothered by the petit-bourgeois habits that for the first time were revealing themselves to me, from the vantage point of my *Luisa Spagnoli* clothes, albeit sale items, and the social privileges I possessed of which I was completely unaware. The one thing that struck me was Massimo's father's great desire to talk about the *Comintern*.[4]

Relations with the family intensified as Massimo and I progressed from cohabitants to married couple, then to parents. The dinners intensified as well: always grand-occasion meals. Even when we dropped in unexpectedly, Massimo's mother would extract from her freezer roasts, ricotta rolls to be heated in the oven with meat sauce, eggplant Parmesan, desserts.

There was strong-arming over Massimo, who was the disputed ground. I feared he would be sucked back into the family, into the dependency, into the delicacies, into the perfectly ironed shirts that never had buttons missing.

She frightened me, but more often she made me furious: because we are too alike, always on the lookout to leave our personal mark on everything concerning our home, our family, our world. She was the favorite aunt of all her nieces and nephews, an accomplished seamstress, cook, and homemaker. Mother. On a dress that only needs a hem, she takes it in, lets it out, adds a dart or removes it, modifies the cuff or the neck, she makes it her own. I do the same with my embroidered sweaters (always with some imperfections because I make them up and don't copy a pattern: I can reconstruct a flavor, not copy a recipe), the way I arrange flowers, wrap a gift, or make a papier-maché doll for Tommaso's birthday. For now I am not as heavy-handed as she is, but in twenty years we'll see.

The "home-makerness" that I keep under control inside of me, relegating it to a circumscribed area of reason, in her becomes bold, aggressive, chaotic, resourceful, pervasive. The apparent irrationality that always causes her to turn the entire kitchen upside down, even for the simplest things—buttered pasta and cutlet, for example—answers to an iron-clad logic, to a making herself busy and needed that resounds threateningly inside of me.

We have made very few compromises with each other.

We came dangerously close to the breaking point several times when we were together, vacationing for a month in the house in Posticciola, her house, built with her energy and her resourcefulness, where everything measures up to standards that I do not share.

Starting with food: there is a fireplace, but the food is never cooked on the coals, but overcooked, reused, redressed, recycled. They linger too long at the table, they eat too much, they worry too much about food. And always pasta, and sauces, and condiments, a cuisine too rich in fats and in proteins that around the time of Tommaso's birth began to cause Massimo health problems.

The more I revealed myself to be foreign and intolerant to all this, the more she tried to lure me in with heavy cream and processed cheese. She had envisioned that house as the hearth where the family could regroup, and I pulled away, outside, planting ivy that without a doubt would attract animals inside, fertilizing the rocks, furiously splitting wood, defiantly taking walks, picking wild asparagus, looking for coffee not brewed at home.

(But she too, who should not have been bending down because of her health, would go out in the fields to gather chicory after she finished her chores, her poor excuse that it was "to save money" ready, as she almost sneaked out of the house. Whenever she has fun, her husband reminds her constantly of everything that according to him might be bad for her.)

When I had an offer to work at a convention in Sardinia I accepted immediately. During that summer, when Tommaso was nine months old, everyone's anxiety over a child who refused to grow was added onto the usual aggravations of Posticciola. Increasingly irritated, grounded in a vision of the world that was still high-spirited and arrogant, I had difficulty curbing my mother-in-law's campaigns, directed in particular at dressing my son "like a little man" and at preventing him from masturbating. So she took cover in the careful search for foods that would ensure a more peaceful sleep for Tommaso, while I tenaciously recorded his continual waking-up as one of the unfortunate—but not unusual—events of life. I would exhaust and calm myself in the children's songs that I would make up for him, singing to quiet us both down and to keep myself awake: ". . . this linden tea with just some honey/slides right down into your tummy/go to sleep my little one/white and red and curly one."

So I left happily, taking the bus to Rome and then an airplane, to make myself feel important, independent, free. This was the confirmation of the value of my work, of the financial contribution that derived from it, of the role outside of motherhood that it bestowed on me.

Massimo called me in the evening at the hotel. While we talked my eyes scanned the double bed that was all for me, and the bathroom things, all for me as well. There were no diapers, no plastic pants, no diaper ointment. Posticciola was far away, the tales that Massimo told me of Tommaso's days were also pleasantly far away: the meals, the sleeping, the smiles.

On the last day, from the loudspeaker of the convention center I was paged for an urgent call. On the phone, Massimo, excited and proud:

"Tommaso just cut his first tooth."

I left in Cagliari my last—perhaps pernicious—illusions of being able to do without the umbilical cord that ties me to my son. Even though Tommaso may be born into the world, I will always find it impossible to deliver him completely from me.

While I emptied my suitcase my mother-in-law smiled at me uncertainly, halfway between relief and distress: I had stepped down from my pedestal, but she did not gloat.

She came down from her pedestal too, for her actions are never casual: for lunch she recycled dry bread in her mother's soup, the poor, simple soup of the town where she was born, revealing for the first time a glimpse of the roots that until that moment she kept hiding underneath heavy cream, processed cheese, sauces, condiments.

MILK SOUP

milk
rice
butter
Parmesan
salt

I cook the rice in the milk with salt and then dress it with butter and cheese.

ONION SOUP

2 lbs. onions
1 T. flour
1 qt. stock
4 oz. fontina cheese, sliced thinly
2 oz. grated Parmesan cheese
1/4 cup whiskey
homemade bread
oil
butter
salt

I cut the onions into large pieces, and cook them in oil and butter until they are golden. I add the flour, blend well, and add the stock. I let it cook on low heat, covered, for about an hour, or until the onion pieces are almost completely pulp. I remove from the heat and add the whiskey. In a baking casserole, I arrange alternating layers of homemade bread sliced thinly, cheeses, onion sauce, beginning and ending with the latter. Before serving, I put it into a hot oven for about ten minutes.

My first home was made up of two rooms, a bathroom, a galley kitchen, and a terrace three times the size of the apartment. When I moved there I owned a bed, a bookcase made from fruit crates, a sofa with particularly aggressive springs, and an electric coffee pot. No cooking stove whatsoever. But it was summer, and it was an orgy of salads, with tuna, with anchovies, with hard-boiled eggs which almost always got stuck in the electric coffee pot.

With the onset of winter, my portable heating stove—fed by wooden beams obtained from a nearby construction site—served me well for potatoes and chestnuts. Finally I got a range from Beatrice. She came from a strange, brilliant, and chaotic family, which had maintained strong ties with their origins in the

Maremma.[5] One brother was a hunter, so boar and game entered into Beatrice's rich and refined cooking in many ways.

Her mother adopted me, worrying that I did not eat enough: when I was at their home for dinner she prepared enormous steaks for me, and through Beatrice she sent me Bavarian cream made with a large number of eggs. A common respect for food united the brothers as well, who protected me, indulged me, and in turn became desirable company.

Talking with Beatrice, going over our childhoods, similar in many ways (the terrible books we both read, *The Iron Talon, The Young Guard, How Steel was Tempered*), I began to think that a Marxist upbringing does not automatically mean freedom. Or happiness.

Beatrice was my first introduction to psychoanalysis: through her eyes I saw the events of 1968, understanding a few things about it, some important. I have used that view of the world since then to make some decisions. At the time though, I used it to understand Beatrice's reasoning when she took a man away from me: from right under my nose, with a heavyhandedness that was unlike her.

After I had left them together, inside the taxi that brought me home, I kept obsessively asking myself why. The answer came to me even before arriving home—the need for affirmation in that moment was more vital for her than anything else—and as if by magic I understood it as a valid reason, and it no longer hurt.

I had trouble falling asleep that night, but when I did, it was a peaceful sleep.

Late the next morning Beatrice was at my door with a pot of onion soup and the look of someone who expects to be turned away.

I lit the oven, set the table, and we sat. I ate voraciously, warm and solicitous toward her lack of appetite. I had discovered the vindictive fierceness of kindness.

CREAM OF POTATO

1 medium onion
1 envelope of potato flakes

2 cups milk
2 cups water
butter
Parmesan
salt
8 oz. small tubular pasta

I sauté the onion, finely chopped, in the oil, then add the milk and water and bring to a boil. I sprinkle in the potato flakes, bring to a boil once again, and add the pasta. After a couple of minutes, I remove the pot from the stove. The pasta will continue to cook in the hot pot without becoming sticky. At the last minute, I flavor the soup with butter and Parmesan.

STRACCIATELLA

1 cup broth
1 egg
1 T. semolina
1 T. Parmesan cheese

When the broth comes to a boil I sprinkle in the semolina. Ten minutes later I add the egg beaten with the Parmesan, I stir well for a minute or two, and serve very hot.

According to a solid and established tradition, my mother was a saint, a heroine, a martyr. She was the stateless daughter of a revolutionary socialist who had died in Russia during the 1905 revolution, and of a Turkish Greek woman who had done her share by carrying bombs in her shopping bag. In other words, she had all the requirements for entering into the history books herself. She was even distantly related to that Dora Kaplan who had tried to assassinate Lenin (a family tie that came at a dear price in Stalin's "reign of terror" and later as well).

Much about my family is written in books: treatises, memoirs, essays, correspondence. The hero, the woman biologist, the agronomists, the nihilists, the historian, the woman secret agent, the enlightened industrialist. Some became a part of history while still living.

It's not enough to make me understand.

My mother too has her book. A sentence in it reads: "In a moment in which I was feeling a little better I took Clara in bed with me, cuddled with her a moment and kissed her. Right away she asked: 'Can we do this again tomorrow?' How easy it is to feel touched, and to lose all one's strength. . . ." Inside me sounds a very vague echo of tenderness, nothing more. In my mind, my mother has always been dead; my father has always been, if not dead, at any rate frail, fatigued, engrossed. I can only imagine the "before," that hidden core that must nonetheless exist somewhere inside me, and I can only tell it like a fairytale.

My father was at the Paris Peace Conference, in the president's box, when they placed a pale blue envelope in his hand. He thought it would be one of the many official messages ". . . unfortunately cannot attend, best wishes . . ." but the message read "LIBERTY BORN ALL WELL HUGS LOLETTA."

(How many names in their lives, Severi and Saunier, Bernard Marina Aldo Liliane, clandestine names, battle names. Loletta was always his affectionate name for her).

It seemed like revenge: after the prison, the years of absence, the not knowing his first two children, now finally this daughter of peace and lawfulness decided to arrive a month early, when he was not there.

But the important thing was that all had gone well: his life's companion was already calling her with the nickname Liberty, faithful to the pact he had made with his brothers. They would choose her other names together; the future was no longer closed off. The military plane would not take long to get to Rome.

He reached the podium, and it was one of his best speeches: the news had filled him with elation. Now that there was another drop in the enormous sea of history and of revolution, he had to fight for her too.

The young Polish officer who was his bodyguard accompanied him in his rounds along the Seine in search, as always, of rare books. They talked about the conference—a bit circumspectly—about literature, about wines. About children. They ate together without looking each other in the eyes too much, they exchanged a few more jokes, then he boarded the airplane for Rome. Did he buy a gift for Loletta?

Prison, danger, and war had taught her to be silent, organized, efficient. No one would have guessed that there was an infant in the house, who furthermore was joining an already large tribe of relatives, all living in the big house with the long hallways.

Loletta's mother, who perhaps still frequented her socialist revolutionaries' clubs, had already conveniently disappeared from circulation, maybe in France, maybe in Palestine. He didn't know, and it was best that he didn't.

Loletta took him by the hand; she was happy for this little girl with a more tranquil future. They leaned over the crib, and together they watched the sleeping baby, delicate like all pre-emies, tiny.

After the last feeding, past midnight, Loletta would walk through the silence of the house and bring him spaghetti Neapolitan style, cold, just the way he liked it. They would exchange a few words, maybe an embrace, then she would go to bed, and he would continue working until the morning light. At night politics remained outside his study, which was soundproofed by books, and he would reopen his dialogue with the classics, with history, and with music.

He and Loletta saw little of each other, but felt so fortunate. . . . After years of almost insurmountable distances, the iron bars, the searches, the secret codes, the death sentences, living in the same house with their daughters seemed almost like a vacation.

Maybe it was because of this sudden lowering of one's defenses after twenty years that Loletta became ill. Certainly the illness seemed to him like something he could not bear.

As always, their iron-clad organization worked: she in the private clinic in Switzerland for experimental, avant-garde therapies for an incurable illness, he at home, at the Ministry, at party headquarters, at conferences, with his little daughter who should have at least a father, since her mother could not be with her.

The little girl was growing without having problems or causing any. She would quietly fall asleep in the Warsaw hotel rooms while he went on with his meetings. He was awkward in helping her into her pajamas: he had only gotten to know his other daughters when they were grown up.

Now, at night he could no longer just work: he wrote to Loletta, without pretending that neither of them knew. His talent as a lucid and rigorous writer did not help at times, and the wastebasket would fill up with aborted attempts at love letters.

For himself he had accepted everything: torture, death, and unresolvable contradictions, and to everything he had been able to give some sense, as though every event, every thought, was a stitch in a great net that embraced the world. Now the net no longer worked, it was not heroic death which lay in wait for them but cancer: a stupid death, a banal one.

Therefore he took his little girl by the hand and they boarded a train, then a propeller airplane, and then big, dark, and silent cars to go visit Loletta.

In the Russian winter, they were still able to have a vacation: hearing again her native language, Loletta spoke easily; he bought her hats, and the little girl enjoyed the snow, the marble inside the metro, the love.

Naturally, they had to part again.

Back at home, he would lose himself in his work, but right now he only had his little girl. He made up stories for her, held her in his arms in the official photos.

During the trip the child became ill: flushed with fever, she huddled in the sleeping car, refusing the unfamiliar foods of the places they were crossing, sweet-and-sour pork, meatballs with prunes.

They were in Vienna, border between two worlds, narrow corridor between east and west. He used all the influence he had on one side and the other, and got what he wanted: a meat broth with *Stracciatella* and an entire packet of Parmesan cheese to flavor it.

With the Parmesan he formed islands and mountains inside the broth: he had to make up another fairy tale, and then the little girl fell asleep. In her sleep the fever began to go down.

He wrapped her in a red blanket, took her in his arms, and we got off the train.

PASTA WITH EGGPLANT

16 oz. pasta (small shells)
2 eggplants
6 San Marzano tomatoes
1 clove garlic
4 basil leaves
4 T. baked ricotta[6]
oil
salt

I slice the eggplants into small rounds and fry them in plenty of oil, then let them drain on brown paper.

To make the sauce I sauté the garlic in oil, then I add the tomatoes, crushed, and the basil. I cook everything for a few minutes on high heat.

I cook the pasta, to which I then add the sauce, the eggplant, and the ricotta, which I have put through a wide-holed sieve.

LEAVENED DOUGH

1 lb. flour
1 cube yeast
1 1/2 cups warm water
1 clove finely chopped garlic
1/2 t. salt
4 T. oil

Sometimes I buy the dough already made, sometimes I make it myself, provided that I have three hours to let it rise.

I mix all ingredients in a bowl (so as not to soil the tabletop), until I have a rather soft and elastic dough. Leaving a little flour on the bottom, I gather the dough into a ball and with a knife I cut an "x" across the top: both a good-luck gesture and an actual help to the leavening process. I cover the bowl with a cloth, and leave it in a warm part of the house. Then—almost always—I spread it directly into the oiled baking dish, pressing it with my fingers, without using either table or rolling pin.

PIZZA WITH EGGPLANT

1 lb. leavened dough
1 lb. eggplant
1 small fresh mozzarella
1 lb. peeled plum tomatoes
1 clove garlic
5 basil leaves
oil
salt

I slice the eggplant lengthwise and fry it. I prepare a sauce with the plum tomatoes, sautéd garlic, basil, and salt, and cook it for a few minutes on high heat.

I place the dough (which is no thicker than 1/4 inch) in a well-oiled baking pan, and spread the sauce over it, then the eggplant, and the mozzarella, grated or finely diced.

I bake in the oven for about twenty minutes, at 450° F.

PIZZA WITH ONIONS

1 lb. leavened dough
2 large onions
1/4 1b. mortadella
8 oz. Tuscan *caciotta*[7]
oil
salt

I roll out the dough, set it on a well-oiled baking sheet, and arrange in order the cheese, grated, then the mortadella, cut into very thin slices, the onion, finely chopped, and a good pinch of salt.

Bake twenty minutes in the oven, at 450° F.

PIZZA WITH GREENS

1 lb. leavened dough
1 lb. steamed greens (chard, spinach, or nettles)

2 oz. tuna in oil

2 oz. olives

2 oz. mixed pickles

a few capers

oil

salt

I chop all the ingredients coarsely and mix them together except, of course, the leavened dough. I make two thin rounds with the dough and I arrange the mixture on the top of one. I cover it with the other one and close the borders pressing them carefully together. I brush the top with oil and pierce it here and there with a fork. I bake it for forty-five minutes at 450° F.

In the seventies, during those elections that we had to follow until dawn to really know how they would turn out, where the results dribble in gradually and without projections, the only solution was these pizzas. I would prepare them while the polls were open, and we would eat them casually as they came out of the oven.

In 1974, for the divorce referendum, I was with all my old friends. There was champagne for a toast and Enrico's hugs full of expectation; the big changes were there, at arm's reach.

In 1975 several things had changed. There was Massimo, and the group: my friends and his were incompatible numbers. My past became like a closed box, set aside, already useless. The critical sense with which I had initially analyzed the group had disappeared, erased by an eagerness to accept and to be accepted.

Paolo and Patrizia were already married, Aldo and Maria lived together: these relationships had a precarious, episodic quality about them, so that my home, established and centrally located, was everyone's meeting point. The profound difference between my cooking and their playing with food, or their refusal to accept it as something to be reckoned with, was already a conflict. The pizza mediated between our different ways, but Aldo either didn't care or simply found it acceptable.

Before the elections, there were discussions and political analyses until late at night. The women, except for Francesca, were silent. Aldo was the leader, Paolo opposed him occasionally and almost casually, without open confrontations.

After a traumatic episode that involved three members of our group, the couples' boundaries appeared clearly staked.

I had been diffident toward the rigidity that dominated everything we did (the interminable clashes to decide between cinema icons such as Fassbinder and Rohmer, to finally compromise with Risi). What I cared about instead, was the possibility of bringing back inside the group the tensions of each couple, and the moral imperative underlying each person's actions.

The night of the elections everyone was there in front of the small fuzzy television, even people who had a marginal and discontinuous relationship with the group, brought in by the magnetic force of a nucleus that was still vital and committed to the revolutions that were to come.

The pizza was not well cooked, but I didn't care either: we were so full of the victory that we were not even hungry. The bottle of wine passed from hand to hand, even among the teetotalers. When we went out, dragged to Via delle Botteghe Oscure by an ancient umbilical cord, our eyes shone.

From the balcony, with a weary smile, Party Secretary Berlinguer urged the crowds to be calm and to reflect.

At the elections in 1976, we were so certain of winning that Aldo agreed to take up a collection for champagne: we put it in the freezer to cool it more quickly, forgot about it, and the bottle burst without cheer.

PASTA WITH BUTTER

10 oz. pasta
4 T. butter
2 oz. Parmesan cheese
salt

Generally viewed as evidence of slovenliness, pasta with butter is rendered respectable by just a few details. The butter should be warmed in the serving bowl along with some of the Parmesan; the pasta must not be completely drained, but rather must retain a small part of the cooking water, which I use to better blend in the rest of the Parmesan.

When I used to hear about him (his nickname constantly came up in conversations) I thought he must be the son of himself, a person whose notoriety belonged to the world of the Fathers, located in History. The forty-year-old who was quoted in the living rooms of the "red" bourgeois society that I frequented could not be that same person.

I met him in January in connection with my work; it dawned on me that these persons were one and the same. He asked of me a complicity that implied a sociopolitical status that, to that point, no one had acknowledged in me, including myself.

We were working shoulder to shoulder. One day in March, he greeted me with a little friendly kiss and already he was turning into the One Great Love: all other relationships erased, burned to ashes and consumed by its burning light.

In May it seemed that the scattered pieces of myself might find each other again: he praised my organizational skills, but also appreciated the fact that I sang at the Folk-Studio, that I lived alone, that I loved France (remembering together a generally obscure Trenet song), and that I wrote.

I acquiesced to food becoming of secondary importance; the only acceptable nourishment was coffee, and without sugar at that. It was not a diet, but a kind of refusal to eat except fortuitously, at a cafeteria or restaurant, at off times, cheerfully.

I had the feeling that he was genuinely curious about me, and he used my talents fully, all of them, and this conferred a sense of my value, even in my own eyes.

He was a father figure: culturally, politically, almost literally. I have loved the lines of his face and of his soul more than his own reality.

In July people had become accustomed to seeing us together. I lived by the telephone, in a sort of desperate and futile availability. But he liked a story I had published right around then, and maybe he would come hear me sing one day soon.

So many restaurants were closed in August. We had to work late, and I got to his place with a package of spaghetti, a stick of butter, and a packet of grated Parmesan.

We sat next to each other to eat, he even said the pasta was good (generally he never passed judgment on food, limiting himself to swallowing it to survive). For a moment it seemed that we might open the bottle of Cordon Rouge in the refrigerator. But already his eyes were far away; he began talking about the issue of the newspaper we were preparing. He disappeared to make a phone call.

Before leaving, I wanted to wash the dishes: his annoyance, my insistence turned almost into a physical clash.

The kiss we exchanged at the door was still a friendly one, not complicitous, though.

PASTA WITH ZUCCHINI

1 lb. zucchini
1 clove garlic
16 oz. short cut pasta (penne, cannolicchi)
oil
salt
I T. grated Parmesan cheese

I grate the zucchini, and while the pasta is cooking I sauté it in a frying pan along with the garlic, finely chopped. I flavor the dish with the Parmesan.

POLENTA WITH THREE CHEESES

8 oz. fine polenta (corn) meal
8 oz. coarse polenta (corn) meal
1 cup milk
4 oz. Gruyère cheese
4 oz. fontina cheese
4 T. butter
2 oz. grated Parmesan cheese

I cook the polenta in a pressure cooker, with salted water and the milk. After the necessary fifteen minutes, I add the fontina and Gruyère, cut into small cubes, the butter and the Parmesan, and let them dissolve for a minute on the heat.

In high school, one day, when one of the teachers was absent, Mr. Celli showed up to substitute. He walked in, and asked us if we had work to do or if we would rather read something together. The question itself came as a surprise. We were used to annoyed substitutes, to teachers who asked only to be left alone.

"Who wants to read? Okay, you go ahead. It's a science fiction story."

He addressed us formally, using *Lei*, and we felt like giggling. Moreover, we considered science fiction fourth-rate reading, along the lines of Mickey Mouse comic strips.

The story was "The Sentinel," forty lines, a new world.

Mr. Celli became a familiar figure in the classroom as a substitute, and in the hallways. He helped us launch our newspaper, which until then had had a very precarious life. He did the same for the film club, the school excursions, the book club, the concerts. The school board tolerated it all, except for a series on Eisenstein.

Mr. Celli was barely over thirty. He had cancer, and knew it.

His eyes were sweet and mature in his unhandsome face. I fell in love with his shabby raincoat, with science fiction, with his adulthood.

For New Year's Eve he invited me to his brother's house. My family gave me permission: for the first time I was doing something that was not with my schoolmates, not with parents that picked us up just after midnight. I felt grown up: my older sisters' parties had only been reflected glory. This invitation was for me.

Climbing the stairs of the apartment in the old part of the city made us out of breath. Inside, the ceiling had wooden beams; a wooden Christmas tree stood decorated with a dangling *Pulcinella* puppet and a few tangerines. Brassens on the record player, thirty-year-olds who didn't treat me like an outsider.

I had fantasized a great deal, ready to sacrifice my life, and above all, that flower of virginity that was beginning to weigh on me. I had fantasized about the food as well: a symbolic banquet would certainly crown my initiation.

We danced cheek to cheek—still using the formal address with each other—his breathing just slightly wheezing next to my ear.

At midnight, toasts and greetings, a small kiss.

It was time to eat: I was expecting maybe caviar and champagne, or perhaps some other kind of food for grown-ups that I couldn't even imagine.

Celli's brother emerged from the kitchen with an enormous wooden board: the polenta narrowed the gap between our spoons and our worlds.

He took me home in a taxi when it was almost morning, holding my hand and still using the formal *Lei*.

4

second courses

EGGPLANT ROLLS

1 lb. white eggplant
1/2 lb. ground meat
1 egg
3 T. fresh breadcrumbs
6 basil leaves
1 16 oz. can whole tomatoes
2 oz. baked ricotta cheese

I cut the eggplant slices lengthwise and fry them in plenty of oil and let them drain on brown paper. I make oblong meatballs—mixing the meat, breadcrumbs, egg, salt, three of the basil leaves—which I place on each eggplant slice and roll them up, securing each roll with a toothpick.

I then prepare a sauce with sautéed chopped garlic, peeled tomatoes, the other three basil leaves, and add the eggplant rolls to it. I simmer the sauce until reduced, turning the rolls gently so as not to break them.

Before serving, I sprinkle each portion with grated baked ricotta.

STUFFED CABBAGE ROLLS

10 cabbage leaves
1/2 lb. ground meat
1 egg
3 T. fresh breadcrumbs
3 T. chopped parsley
1 lb. peeled tomatoes

1 large onion minced

salt

pepper

oil

I blanch the cabbage leaves until flexible, but not too soft. I mix the meat, egg, breadcrumbs, parsley, salt, and pepper and place equal parts of the mixture on each cabbage leaf, which then is rolled and secured with a toothpick. At this point, I sauté the onion in a little oil, then add the tomatoes, and cook just enough to thicken slightly. It is now time to immerse the cabbage rolls in the sauce and cook uncovered for about twenty minutes.

At the beginning of the fifties my family was a normal family: for the first time a father, a mother, three daughters, all living together in the same house. Each daughter's nickname was a tie to the past that was still close: Ada, the oldest, was called 'Ottobrina' after the October Russian revolution and was the "daughter of clandestine life." Giulia was still "the daughter of war," and I—the youngest—was (for the moment) the "daughter of peace." The considerable age differences between us reflected the years my father spent in prison, first in the nation's jails, then in the Nazi ones.

Also part of our normal ménage were a full time maid, Aunt Ermelinda, and Grandmothers Alfonsa and Xenia who from time to time would arrive from Palestine.

The photos of Ada's wedding show a family only slightly unusual: a civil ceremony, the bride in a suit with a gardenia and a luminous smile, my father toothless and still emaciated from the war, Giulia with a sort of frightened look on her face that has never completely disappeared, myself as a three-year-old girl. My mother is still beautiful, but her eyes are already weary.

An image of short-lived family unity; a year later Ada and her husband landed eventfully in Czechoslovakia, and my mother started her pilgrimage to the private clinics where her life was going to end: Valdoni, the Soviet Union, Lausanne. From time to time she would be back home—it was clear that each time could be the last—and the family would again resume its normality: the fir tree with its lights on New Year's Day, the dining table next to the green velvet living room set, my father less barricaded in his study. But those were sporadic episodes. Therefore, when my mother died, she had long been dead for me, and my early childhood was set on a track that did not anticipate her presence.

She left behind a difficult name (none of my report cards show an accurate spelling), a reputation as a courageous woman who loved beautiful things that she never in her adventurous life possessed, and as a woman of sensitivity and of fine taste, capable, like Scarlet O'Hara, of making a dress out of draperies. And as a poor cook.

I like to think that the stuffed cabbage leaves—a Slavic tradition I believe—come from her, but that doesn't really mean that it is so. It is uncertain, like all the other things about her life that have come down to me.

CHICKEN WITH SOY SAUCE

1 whole chicken breast (boneless)
2 T. port wine
2 T. soy sauce
2 T. cornstarch
2 handfuls soy sprouts
vegetable oil

I flatten the chicken breast and slice it into several thin slices. I cook the slices two or three minutes in hot oil, then add the cornstarch dissolved in the soy sauce and the port. I let the sauce thicken on low heat, add the soy sprouts, and keep cooking for no more than two minutes.

CHICKEN WITH CHESTNUTS

1 whole chicken
10–15 chestnuts
1/4 cup brandy
1 bay leaf
butter
salt

I place the shelled chestnuts inside the already cleaned cavity of the chicken, along with a good pinch of salt, the brandy, and the crumbled bay leaf.

I butter the surface of the chicken and sprinkle it with salt and I bake it for about an hour at 480° F., turning it around from time to time to let it brown on all sides.

VILLEROY CHICKEN

roast chicken leftovers
thick béchamel sauce
flour and 1 beaten egg
oil for frying

I try to give a flat, regular shape to the chicken leftovers. I then dip the pieces in the béchamel sauce, which must be cold, then dredge them in flour and dip in the beaten egg. I fry them in abundant oil. They are very good either hot or cold.

CHICKEN IN A SALT CRUST

1 whole chicken, cleaned
10 lbs. coarse salt

On a sheet of foil I place half of the salt in a mound and make a well, placing the chicken in the center, and cover it completely with the rest of the salt, forming a round mound. I close up the foil and bake it for two hours at 480° F. I remove the foil and use a hammer to break the crust around the chicken, which comes out dry, fatless, and not at all salty.

MEATLOAF BAKED IN FOIL

1 boneless, whole chicken breast, cut into thin slices
1 lb. of ground meat
4 T. breadcrumbs
1 raw egg + 1 hard-boiled egg
chopped parsley
1 garlic clove
1 carrot
salt

I combine the meat with the raw egg, breadcrumbs, chopped garlic, parsley, and salt. I spread the mixture out on foil in a single layer, about 1/2-inch thick, and then arrange the chicken slices, carrot, and hard-boiled egg over the surface. I roll this up so that all the other ingredients are sealed inside, then I close the foil all around and bake for an hour at 430° F.

When I was an adolescent the term "anorexia" was not yet fashionable; that must have been the reason why my fasting did not carry serious consequences. I was, however, always very thin (in the snapshots of that time knees, elbows, feet are most prominent) and my last period of life at home with my parents was marked by a radical refusal of food; I was throwing up almost everything I ate.

The family doctor diagnosed colitis and put me on a diet: no fat, no bread. When the maid took her week of vacation and we divided the chores among us, as had happened before, I got to do the cooking.

I liked cooking, especially sweets and custards, and whipping the butter for the tarts, everything that had a scent of richness and superfluous things. I had been doing this since I was little, and as an adult I always leaned toward adding an extra touch (often too much) to everyday cooking.

Those extra touches were gone once I started following a diet, which also meant an unusual closeness to my father, who was on a perpetual diet and whose taste was notoriously in opposition to mine. My mother, who did not enjoy cooking, was doomed, knowing all too certainly that if one of us liked a dish, the other would undoubtedly have declared it inedible.

My sister Giulia, meanwhile, convinced that she needed to lose weight, took refuge behind enormous dishes of undressed salad.

I wanted to demonstrate, (I don't know to whom: my father, my mother, or whomever) that I was able to cook well, even with no fat.

The first day I made the chicken in salt, which I brought defiantly to the table.

My father ate it while talking about other things, without commenting about it. Then, at the end: "Not bad. This is similar to the chicken-in-a-paper-case *mammà* used to make."

I was waiting, holding my breath.

"But . . ."—he kept on, holding up his fork, and that "but" was suspended in mid-air like Damocles' sword, the habitual critique assigned to my mother's culinary efforts as well—"but something is missing . . . I have it: perhaps you should have put some crushed garlic on it . . ." I hated garlic, I hated those "buts."

We had a garden, and in the summer we often ate outside. I spent the second day of my kitchen assignment gathering pinecones and dry twigs, then toward the evening I made a fire and set up the grill. I marinated the steaks, and added one clove of garlic, no more.

We sat at the table and the objection arrived as expected: the salt, how many times have I told you, the salt has to be put in afterwards, otherwise the meat gets tough. I swallowed garlic and rage.

The third day I took a big risk, which was almost a provocation: I prepared stuffed zucchini as Grandmother did, the *mammà* who, from what I could remember, knew how to cook only a few things, but whose culinary art was nevertheless unsurpassed in my father's memory.

The "but" arrived once more, I don't remember about what. I ate with false appetite, obstinate, thinking without the courage to say so, that my zucchini was better than Grandmother's.

That night I had a colic attack and threw up everything: it must have been the oil I used to fry the zucchini, suggested Giulia, as she held my head. She looked powerless and sorrowful, unable to mediate between her divided loyalties.

Exhausted, with black circles under my eyes, the next morning I faced my fourth day in the kitchen.

I consulted every cookbook in the house in my attempt to prevent my father's "but." All my life, under my father's gaze, there was an unavoidable "but," and each of my attempts to assert independence, freedom, take an intellectual position, would clash against his fury, or a conceited smile. In his greener years he had done, and better than I, all the things I was trying to do: studying, establishing relationships, politics, even cooking. (I passionately hated the Neapolitan-style tomato sauce he made, his boasted and very simple piece of *bravura* which to this day I have still to accept.)

Maybe he wanted me to take different routes from his. But it was not easy to avoid encroaching on his territory: he had done and knew so many things. And thus I had no other choice but to venture beyond the borders again and again, in my choice of academic subjects, in my different ways of looking at politics, in preparing his *mammà*'s zucchini.

On that fourth day of my kitchen duties, I decided—I don't know how consciously, and whether out of fear or courage—not to venture too far.

I prepared a mixture for meatballs (without Parmesan cheese otherwise he would tell me that there was a taste of "dead cow"), which I spread on a sheet of foil and covered with a carrot, hard-boiled egg, and chicken breast. I rolled it up, sealed in foil and put it in the oven dreaming of glory and revenge during the entire baking time. When it was done, I let it cool down and sliced it carefully.

In front of those slices I lost heart. They looked like aspic, like Grandmother's stuffed chicken.

By then it was too late. The mosaic effect of the carrot, egg, chicken, and beef displayed itself attractively on the serving dish; there was no way to conceal it. I even added some salad leaves for decoration and brought it to the table as if I were going to the gallows.

"This is good," pronounced my father. "Where did you find the recipe?"

"I made it up," I answered without hesitation.

Too defeated to display my usual provocative style, I lowered my head, expecting a hailstorm of "buts."

"Really good," my father concluded.

I went to my room and cried all my tears.

STUFFED ZUCCHINI

8 rather large zucchini
1 lb. ground beef
1 egg
3 T. fresh breadcrumbs
1 T. grated Parmesan cheese

1 T. chopped parsley
1 clove of garlic, minced
oil
salt

I halve the zucchini lengthwise and gently scrape out the insides (which can be utilized later for omelet). I combine all other ingredients except the oil, and fill the cavity of the zucchini with this mixture. I then sprinkle a little oil on each and place them on a well-oiled baking dish. I let them bake at 425° F. for about an hour. Can be eaten warm or cool.

SAVORY MEATBALLS

1 lb. ground meat
3 T. fresh breadcrumbs
2 T. grated Parmesan cheese
1 egg
2 celery stalks
2 large onions
3 medium carrots
1 sprig parsley
oil
salt

I thoroughly mix the meat, egg, Parmesan, and breadcrumbs, and shape the mixture into meatballs. In a large frying pan I sauté all the vegetables and parsley, coarsely chopped, in plenty of oil. When the onions start to become translucent, I add the meatballs and cook on low heat, moistening them with a little white wine.

SMALL MEATBALLS WITH CURRY

1 lb. ground meat
4 T. fresh breadcrumbs
2 T. Parmesan cheese
1 egg
2 large onions
curry

1 T. cornstarch or potato starch
1 cup stock
oil
salt

I combine the meat, breadcrumbs, Parmesan, egg, salt, and a first pinch of curry, and form small balls slightly larger than a hazelnut. I sauté together the coarsely chopped onions and the meatballs, then I blend in the starch and add the stock along with four or five good pinches of curry. I let it simmer for half an hour.

STUFFED PEPPERS

8 medium-sized red and yellow sweet peppers
3/4 lb. ground meat
1 egg
1 stale bread roll
1 cup milk
1 clove garlic
parsley
basil
oil
salt

I dip the bread in warm milk, squeeze it well, and mix it together with the meat, egg, garlic, chopped parsley, basil, and salt. I remove the stem and seeds from the peppers, making sure I don't break the shell. After salting them inside, I fill each pepper halfway with the mixture to which I have added a few pieces of sweet pepper.

I salt the peppers outside as well, place them in a well-oiled baking dish, and bake at 430° F. for about forty minutes, turning them once or twice as they cook.

How generally ugly and messy were the relationships between us sisters! Ada could be my mother, Micol could be my daughter; Giulia and Stefania have tried to establish relationships with me in which I have always disappointed them.

Periodically (but never all together), we attempted to weave stronger ties with each other; a coupling based on a common mother has had some results: Ada-Giulia, Stefania-Micol.

I think it is because of my intermediate position of being equidistant in age and affection (a proximity that never reaches close enough to touch), that I feel as if these roots, these ties, do not belong to me, nor do they give me any guarantees. Having two mothers doesn't mean doubled love, having four sisters doesn't mean a big family. The only road I can travel is that of regret kept under control, a daily practice of resignation with which I try to drive away anger and resentment.

But I cannot accept being resigned about Micol: I'm still looking for openings, although I expect they will be impossible. (Calling her Micol is also a way of not surrendering: she has another name. When she was born my father registered her under five names—the maximum allowed by the law—but he did not give her this biblical name which I proposed, strong in my pride and curiosity about our Jewish roots.)

Being a Jew and a Marxist, an implacable and searing need for coherence demanded not only his rejection of Zionism, but also that he be the first to sign a parliamentary petition against the state of Israel. But along with this side of him, there was also his ironic and touching use of certain terms from the ghetto, such as when he would refer to somebody as "a real *negro di canapetta.*"[1] Consequently, the term *negritude* was always an ambiguous word with him, suspended between an emancipating impetus and the Judaic-Roman slang.

Micol has a head full of curls, big eyes, and the soft, athletic body of a *Sabra* soldier: the first to define her—obviously pleased—"the Jewess of the house" was our father.

When she was born I was already grown up, too old to be jealous of her. She had a father who could be her grandfather and a mother absorbed by his ills: taking care of her was of little cost to me; I was fascinated with playing mother and daughter.

Micol was frail. It took her hours to finish a bottle, after which I would lay her on top of me, her naked tummy against my own bare stomach because she was always cold, listless, born in a difficult moment of our lives: my father was convalescing from a heart attack and was kept on morphine; his eyes were glazed and we were not to cross him.

The emergency that temporarily kept my mother away from Micol ended, and Micol was dutifully returned to her. The daughter's jealousy turned into mother's jealousy. I was trying to nurture a special relationship with Micol, spoiling and indulging her. She had difficulty sleeping, and at times I would take her in bed with me.

When I left home, the only deep pain I felt was because of Micol. She was three years old and thanks to me, in part, she had become soft and round. I felt I was abandoning her in a hostile land, and I was afraid she would forget me.

Distrustful, Micol refused for a long time to come to the houses where I lived. When she finally came I wanted to make a special dinner for her, but I fell back on pasta with butter, ground veal, and bananas. Because she had had such a difficult time with food from the time she was a baby (and with other things too I suppose), she still hung on to simple, monotonous food. At most one could cajole her, from time to time, into tasting something new, which she would approach as if it were medicine.

An emergency called me back home: my mother was once again away, and I found myself with my father and Micol, who became ill. I rubbed her chest; she had the funny-looking body of a twelve year old, neither fish nor fowl, the back of an adolescent boy, the tummy of a child. I found myself feeding her again, when she was exhausted by fever. We established once again a rapport of physicality, but I don't know how much she trusted me. The family doctor was coming almost every day. He was at his wits' end and commented: "See how difficult it is to be a mother?"

The emergency past, I turned the responsibilities over to her legitimate mother and went back to my home and the life of a single woman, away again from Micol. I was the one to go see her, because she almost never agreed to go out with me. Her only passion was *gianduiotti* chocolates, which I would give her any time I could afford them.

My mother continued patiently her educational task with Micol: with a bit of this and a bit of that, Micol's nutritional horizon started to expand. Small steps, always with basically insipid food, potatoes, chicken, zucchini.

As an adult, one day, Micol began to tell me with effort about herself; maybe she thought I could be a sister to her. She handed me her suffering made of old resentments and recent pains; the shield she kept around her fell suddenly; she was naked and defenseless, and wounded. Perhaps we were finally together; she, in an armchair, and I on the sofa, we sat and talked about where to go from there.

I had sweet peppers for dinner, too strongly flavored to even think of proposing them to her. She did not stay to eat but wanted to try them, and she liked them.

And maybe we felt a bit more like sisters when she called me from home and asked for the recipe.

MEATLOAF WITH NETTLES

1 bunch nettles
1 lb. lean ground meat
4 cups stock
1 cup mayonnaise

I put the nettles and ground meat in the stock and bring to a brisk boil. When cooked, I drain and squeeze the mixture well, then place it in a serving dish and shape it into a loaf. When it has cooled I cover it with mayonnaise.

When I left home everything was easy: on one side stood university, family, oppression, the feeling of not being able to take it any longer, the fear; on the other was work, taking risks, breathing new air.

I earned little, ate everything that was available to me (from cough drops to sugar packets stolen from coffee shops), and stopped having colic even though I lived on canned foods. Freedom made me gain weight: my angular body made of knees and elbows began to soften.

At the beginning I had a furnished room in Trastevere, with a deaf landlady who filled the room with fake birds inside gilded cages and who forbade me to use hot water. During the long walks I took to save on bus fare, I discovered that the sky wasn't there simply to figure out whether or not I needed an umbrella.

Paola had red hair, and was a few years older than I. Unlike other colleagues who were looking suspiciously at my choices, she accepted them instead as normal. Her mother had died not too long before. When her father remarried she put him and the step-mother out and remained mistress of the house, which she opened up to me.

In the morning we would leave the house together in her car, a dilapidated "Bianchina." She taught me how to rinse the silver-ware well, how to save on the hairdresser, and especially how to recycle leftovers and make them edible, something that has not yet lost its usefulness for me, and which I later defined as "cook-ing table corners."

At the end of the month, when our finances were nearly exhausted and batter for frying was a great resource, we would use it for Parmesan cheese rinds and minuscule vegetable leftovers.

With our new paycheck we allowed ourselves one afternoon at the supermarket; we would look around and around. Finally we would not buy much but always picked up something frivo-lous, a nonessential, expensive food to make all the rest tolerable: a tube of salmon paste, cheese crackers, a little cream.

In the kitchen we took turns cooking for each other. It was a common language. Making a meatloaf, for example, was not just assembling the ingredients, it meant creating a lacework of pars-ley, carrots, and olives on the mayonnaise. It also gave us a good excuse for running to the farthest open fields at the edge of the city in search of herbs and an outing.

We talked about our mothers. Her adolescence appeared to me different and enviable; I projected on her a strength I would never possess. Compared to my totally absent family, Paola's father allowed her to skillfully trade on his guilt, as he gave her the frivolous presents I longed for from mine.

One day the phone rang, I was asleep:

"Hello honey, this is daddy, how are you?"

Stunned and sleepy I felt a moment of happy illusion, then I got up and went to call her.

BOILED MEAT WITH GREEN SAUCE

1 1/4 lb. beef brisket
1 bone (knee)
2 bouillon cubes

2 carrots

1 celery rib

1 onion with 1 clove pressed into it

For the green sauce:

1 bunch of parsley

a handful of salted capers

1 garlic clove

1 t. anchovy paste

oil

I put the meat, the vegetables and spices (the clove pressed into the onion) in boiling water. Meanwhile I prepare the green sauce by chopping the garlic, parsley, and rinsed capers very finely. I put all this in a small bowl, add the anchovy paste, and start drizzling the oil into it, mixing well and whipping as if it were mayonnaise.

Before bringing it to the table, I let the boiled meat cool almost completely, and serve it with the green sauce.

GARNISHED BOILED MEAT

1 lb. beef brisket

1 half chicken

1 beef knee bone

2 bouillon cubes

2 carrots

1 celery rib

1 onion with one clove pressed into it

2 egg whites

1/4 cup dry Marsala wine

2 or 3 sheets of hard gelatin (can be substituted with 2
    envelopes of unflavored gelatin)

For the dressing:

hard-boiled eggs

mayonnaise

olives

pickles

capers

raw carrots

I place the meat in a pressure cooker filled with cold water together with the bone, vegetables, and bouillon. After letting it boil for one hour, I add the chicken, and let it cook for another twenty minutes or so. I remove the meat from the stock, which I place in the refrigerator to cool.

After a few hours, I skim the already-thick film of fat from the stock. I beat the egg whites in a pan, add the Marsala wine, the stock, and heat the mixture up while continuing to whip. I also add the gelatin sheets that I have softened in warm water. When the mixture is dense and starts to float to the top, I sieve the gelatin through a piece of cheesecloth and it is ready to be used.

I cut the chicken and the meat into small pieces, discarding fat, bones, and skin, and I start arranging meat, pickles, and mayonnaise on the bottom of a rather large baking dish. When it is all arranged I cover it with the cooled gelatin and put it in the refrigerator for at least two hours.

Just before bringing to the table, I warm up the baking dish in a pan of hot water (just enough for the gelatin to detach from the dish) and turn it onto a serving platter.

In Aldo and Maria's home there was a fixed menu: overcooked pasta and ascetic, unflavored omelets, a maximum of frugality, a minimum of time spent in the kitchen. To be able to serve the "people" meant that one had to adjust to their lowest and most uneducated standards, a norm that the group never dared to challenge.

In my home, I had stopped offering choice delicacies: even though everyone was eating with gusto, Aldo had noted my bourgeois attitude.

I was not yet thinking of an open confrontation with him. I was seeking alliances, even basic ones; incapable of breaking their male solidarity, I tried to get Massimo on my side.

Aldo appreciated my sense of autonomy but I wanted him to love me. He rejected me, saying that he was interested only in either very beautiful or very militant women. There was no room for me; the only possibility left was to find a middle ground.

I made the French cheese, good wine, and carefully selected breads disappear; the boiled meat was inexpensive, and I thought it might be acceptable to them. The colorful pickles and the mayonnaise designs made it more tolerable to me.

Aldo said:

"You must have spent all day at it."

We ate, but nobody commented on how it tasted.

Then came the aborted attempts to make small talk. By now I was not the only one in the group to feel like discussing something other than politics; instead of the usual examination of world events, this time we started to sing. We knew how to sing the songs of the struggle together; we savored the pleasure of the music made by many, surprised at times by some lovely harmonies.

One song though, *Contessa*, we didn't feel we could sing again: it sounded strident and far removed in history. Instead, we slipped into a sixties revival; the impossibility of the project we had set out for ourselves became clear to us in the discordant choruses that sucked us into the past.

BEEF STEW WITH TARRAGON

1 1/2 lbs. beef cut into small pieces
1/2 cup white wine
1/2 cup aromatic vinegar
1/2 t. fresh or dry tarragon
1 garlic clove
oil
salt

After sautéeing the crushed garlic in the oil, I add the meat, which I let cook over high heat for ten minutes until lightly browned. I then add tarragon, wine, vinegar, and salt, and let it simmer, covered, for at least one hour.

It was my turn to provide the dinner at Tommaso's preschool. The meat was the best, the sauce thickened to the right point. I looked with satisfaction at the forty children chewing and even swallowing, something not to be taken for granted. They asked me what the pieces of herbs in the sauce were, and foolishly I said *dragoncello*[2] (tarragon). A sort of electric charge snaked around the tables; it looked as if I had evoked the personal dragon that haunted each child's nights.

They started to get up, agitated.

Carlo stayed at his place, serious and thoughtful; I wished he would keep eating, his example helping to reestablish some kind of order.

How wrong I was! Carlo gave me an adult look of sadness: dragons were his friends, he told me, the only ones he could count on besides spaceships, therefore he would never use them for his nourishment, he was no cannibal.

Nobody was eating anymore, all the experience and effort of the teachers seemed ineffectual to save the situation. I had the idea of saying that *dragoncello* was an *anti*-dragon herb. We made up a song about it, persuading them slowly until they started eating again.

Everyone but Carlo: he kept defending his dragon, he did not want to send it away, the pain in his eyes was tangible and at the same time inaccessible.

He even refused dessert: he walked out all by himself into the schoolyard looking for the Big Bad Wolf, another beloved friend of his.

BEEF STEW WITH MILK

1 1/2 lb. stew meat cut into small pieces
1 cup vinegar
2 cups milk
1/2 t. fresh or dry tarragon
1 garlic clove
oil
salt

I sauté the sliced garlic in the oil, add the meat and let it brown. After about ten minutes, I add the milk, vinegar, tarragon, and salt and let it cook covered over low heat for at least one hour.

At the very end, if there is a lot of liquid, I let the sauce thicken: it must cover the meat thickly, like heavy cream.

BEEF STEW WITH JUNIPER

1 1/2 lb. beef cut into small pieces
1/2 cup vinegar
1/2 cup white wine
8 juniper berries
1 garlic clove
oil
salt

After I sauté the garlic in the oil, I brown the meat, adding the crushed juniper berries. After ten minutes, I add wine and vinegar, and let it cook covered for one hour. I add the salt only in the last ten minutes.

VEAL ROAST WITH ONIONS

1 1/2 to 1 3/4 lb. lean veal
2 lbs. onions
1 cup wine
1 cup stock
oil
salt

I cut the onions in large chunks and let them brown in plenty of oil. I add the meat and let it brown, and then start adding stock and wine, alternately, until the meat is cooked (about an hour and a half, over medium low heat).

In the summer of my fifteenth year I attempted suicide for the first time. While I was in the hospital, I saw my mother crying—a luxury she indulged in, as I recall, no more than four times in thirty years.

After the usual stomach pumping and IV, they gave me a lecture. They told me about the dangers I had miraculously escaped and of my having to deal with the police as well as the psychiatrist. Then they sent me to the seaside with two sisters, one older, the other younger. During that month my father and mother came to visit for one day; Micol was in the baby carrier, just a few months old. Always attracted to technological gadgets, my father had bought a movie camera. He used the wrong exposure and the movie turned out to be all soft-focused and beautiful: Micol sitting squat on my shoulder, a relationship suspended in tonality from red to orange, real in its artificiality.

I believe that, as always, the apparent reason for my discomfort was an unhappy love. A happy love—for example, a loving friendship that is now going on almost twenty years—is something about which, after all, there is very little to say.

Strengthened by the sea air, my healthy body responded, and I fell in love, reciprocated, with Francone, a classmate. A love without pain.

Tall and a bit heavy, in ninth grade he was already shaving every day. The teachers treated him with the sort of haughtiness reserved for those who had been held back a year until he declared, by revealing his birth date, that he was in the right grade for his age. He had big, soft arms, a good bulwark against the world.

Together on the beach, together on the paddleboat, together braving the storm on the pier around the castle. One night while leaning up against the walls of a house kissing in a manner inappropriate in those times, we got a bucketful of water dumped on us. At our house—Giulia and Stefania were out, strolling somewhere—Francone dried his pants with the iron, modestly shrouded in my blue kimono, which did not even come down to his knees.

Perhaps I caused him pain; I was too involved, as I sometimes was, with my own suffering to be able to care about his.

In our school, dominated by right-wing organizations and the Catholic Youth Group, what brought us together was a feeling of being confusedly Communist. We created a newsletter that later was called *Ulysses*. By July, we had already printed the proofs on my father's ditto machine. To all of us, sex was in the nebulous future, modulated in the notes of the popular song *A Summer Place* that enabled us to experience it vicariously. Our dreams of independence were limited to a home where parents might disappear for a few hours, and this was what I had in mind in organizing my birthday party: a mid-day dinner, (supper was an unthinkable hypothesis, as being back home at eight was a rigid curfew that applied even to the boys) prepared together with other classmates who were vacationing in the same area.

Before disappearing, my sister Giulia prepared a roast for us. The family had always viewed her cooking career with little hope, but she had already tested the roast with onions at various times. I asked her to let it burn around the edges a bit, just the way I liked it, then I expelled her from the house with firm orders not to come back until evening. Giulia started off downtown holding Stefania by the hand, promising her rides and ice cream.

I began the laborious preparation of the mashed potatoes to go with the roast, which we could shape into little wells to hold bits of meat and gravy.

It was a day of ups and downs. We all pretended to know about ingredients and quantities, but at various times I despaired about the outcome: we looked at the green-enameled casserole containing the roast as the only guarantee of a birthday celebration.

The mashed potatoes took the entire morning to make, but in the end we were able to get the hang of it. There was only the roast to slice. I lifted the lid and in front of my eyes stood a little charred stump: out of love or insecurity, because of that wall that stood between us, Giulia had taken too seriously my craving for that "little burned flavor."

We could still use the gravy: Francone cut large slices of homemade bread. It was a very wonderful birthday.

VITELLO TONNATO (VEAL WITH TUNA)

1 1/2 to 1 3/4 lbs. of veal rump
2 onions
1 handful salted capers
4 anchovy filets
1 cup white wine
1 cup vinegar
1 1/2 cups tuna in oil
1 cup mayonnaise

I combine all ingredients, except for the mayonnaise, inside a pressure cooker, and cook for one hour. After removing the meat,

I let the broth evaporate, reducing it to a small quantity, then pass everything through a sieve. I let the sauce sit in the refrigerator for twenty-four hours together with the meat. When it is time to serve it, I slice the meat and cover it with the sauce into which I have already blended the mayonnaise.

The restaurant at the Bologna train station was no less squalid than the others. My father and I were eating quietly: he was irritated with me for being late. Or maybe he was tired because he was returning from a political campaign rally—one of those exertions the doctors had forbidden to no avail.

The menu, evoking the rich cuisine of the Emilia Romagna region, had little appeal for me, but at the bottom, *vitello tonnato* was written in by hand. If I had read *vitel tonné* I would never have chosen it; my Francophile snobbism wouldn't have allowed me to.

Back in Rome, I forced my mother to make several attempts at reproducing the dish, but it took years of trials and a collage of recipes to capture the same taste of the *vitello tonnato* at the Bologna station. I got it right by myself, by chance, one day when, being short of wine, I ended up using some vinegar instead.

Vitello tonnato is not the poor medley of flavors generally offered in restaurants (dry leftovers of veal roast covered with mayonnaise and a distant scent of tuna); it is a golden balance, a concert whose notes must each have their own precise value.

The first time I made the dish, I had my future in-laws for dinner. My father-in-law ate suspiciously (I didn't yet know of his grounded distrust for gastronomic innovations). At the end he said:

"Hmm, this isn't bad, though."

While he also had—still has—his "hmms," his are different; even when they irritate me they are endearing. My father used his "buts" to exorcise feelings, crushing them under the name of the Party or History, even the history of nutrition. To my father-in-law, who fled at twelve from an ungrateful stepmother and life in a harsh countryside, his wife's dishes, which he calls by imaginative names, represent his security, his awkward, harmless defense against the world.

TUNA AND POTATO LOAF

1 1/2 cups tuna in oil
1 1/2 cups cooked potatoes
1 garlic clove, finely sliced
2 T. chopped parsley
1 cup mayonnaise for dressing

I energetically mix tuna, potatoes, garlic, and parsley. I give the mixture the shape of a fish, and then cover it with the mayonnaise.

Decorations and garnishes are up to one's inspiration, mood, and the time at one's disposal.

TUNA LOAF

1 1/2 cups tuna in oil
2 eggs
3 T. Parmesan cheese
juice of one lemon
2 T. fresh breadcrumbs

I combine the ingredients, which I wrap together sausage-like in a cloth napkin tied at the two ends. I let it cook in salted, boiling water for one hour, then drain it and let cool putting a small weight on the top (the small board used to crush herbs and spices, or a toy iron). I serve the dish with mayonnaise and salted capers.

By Christmastime Massimo and I had been living together for a while. Therefore, the fact that he disappeared for three days struck me as something inexplicable. But I still had my habits of independence: I had dinner with my family and otherwise managed well enough.

The following year, our relationship was official: his parents didn't know how to introduce me, ("Massimo's fiancé" didn't sound good to them either, and I found it intolerable). Anyhow, I was invited.

It was a shock for me, and I immediately christened it "the three-day marathon": an endless period of time spent eating, playing cards, then eating again, playing cards, without end, almost without sleeping, from the big Christmas eve supper through the entire night of Saint Stephen (the day after Christmas).

They all seemed crazy to me: brothers, cousins, uncles, nephews, and nieces smothered under the same roof, a patriarchal rite that exposed old wounds and recent ill-feelings.

My intolerance grew with the passing years: there were always more of us (reluctantly, I put myself in that number), and the menu was staunchly identical from one year to the next. My mother-in-law would not modify her fried food platters, whose quality decreased with every reappearance, stone cold, at every meal, and even between card games.

Same place, same people, same menu: I am not used to rituals, and that one seemed to me devoid of any function. Family life (the warm and embracing kind that I never had, that somehow I had both envied and escaped) was reproposed to me in all its suffocating fierceness, its roles branded with fire on each member's skin; the parents were the repositories of power even when their children were past thirty. Massimo was always and ultimately a son and nothing more. Where did we stand as individuals?

I kept myself on the margins, I willed myself outside, concerned to preserve my identity from that magma where my contours and physiognomy would have melted away. They respected me; I doubted they could love me.

On Christmas morning I was still going to my parents' house for presents and dinner; I found the frigid atmosphere invigorating and relaxing compared to what was awaiting me at the other house. I thought that my family, unlike the other one, had left me free to stand on my own two feet.

There was one Christmas without the patriarch; Massimo's father was hospitalized. Even I missed his authority: a man proud of his strength, like all the others of his species. I was beginning, however, to appreciate his generosity, his becoming upset at the weakness of others. Little by little the shapeless mass that was his family began to take form. I began to see, for instance, that my mother-in-law's busyness in the kitchen was an attempt to resist the destructive and vulgar encroaching of couples too caught up in their neurotic and immoral privacy.

But I tenaciously refused assimilation. I tried to beat them by moving the "three day marathon" to my house for once; they let me do it, confident of their strength. They even consented to the addition of my tuna loaf to their firmly established menu. My mother-in-law rearranged all my pots, silverware, and dishes, and in order to find anything I had to ask her.

I realized that they were starting to love me, to consider me one of them: but their affection was too invasive, too warm, too protective, and I clung for dear life to my being strong and independent, intellectual and atheist. Different.

Little by little, with some effort, along the way, I came to understand their reasoning. For their chain of solidarity and affection is not so different from that interest in the world which made me reject family and life as a couple, only to realize later that even these are part of it. In order for the foliage to burst open it is not necessary to cut off trunk and roots.

They were right. I know it from my son Tommaso, for whom the "three-day Christmas marathon" is the greatest event of the year, full of warmth in spite of disagreements and consumerism. I know it for myself, because when the patriarch's illnesses threatened the ritual, I began taking charge of the big Christmas Eve supper. With my tuna loaf, naturally, but also with the fried food, and with all the other nonnegotiable dishes of the unmodifiable menu.

SAUSAGES WITH SWEET PEPPERS

6 sausages
4 sweet peppers
1 garlic clove
oil
salt

I clean the peppers and cut them into thin slices. I cook them in hot oil (in which I have sautéed the garlic) with the sausages cut into two or three chunks. Cooking time: twenty minutes.

I was invited to sing during a celebration of the Festa dell'Unità (May Day) in a town in the province of Reggio Calabria.

I was very hesitant. It was 1973 and my relationship with the Party, never too easy, had progressively rarefied. In addition, it seemed to me that the era of songs was over, and that a dialogue with the party of Gramsci-Togliatti-Longo-Berlinguer (and my father), was no longer possible.

In the end I accepted because they were paying me, and because I was curious to see a small town in the Sila Mountains of Calabria.

I traveled by night. In Reggio, the next morning, half asleep, I reviewed the program pasted on my guitar: one hour of songs about the status of women, about mental institutions and state-approved slaughter.

The comrade from Reggio loaded me into his car and we left: up along mountain roads, sucking lozenges for my voice, until we reached the mural that signaled the entrance to the town.

I had imagined a democratic municipality where the Festa dell'Unità was practically a clandestine undertaking; I found myself in a community celebrating its festival in a sea of red flags: at least one hanging on every electric pole, on every flower pot outside the windows. Women were standing by the doors with rows of food and beverages to share.

The mayor led me to the stage.

All the men were there in the middle of the horseshoe square enclosed by houses. The show had already started: a band was playing among general indifference. Until a female singer arrived: certainly she was not extraordinary, but neither was she so inept as to justify the pandemonium that immediately broke out.

The young woman in slacks courageously sang a couple of songs amid the public hissing. Then she gave up: the square was in an uproar, and insults were flying about. Even the women started to inch toward the edges of the square, their faces disapproving.

I thought that such a politicized town was simply refusing the popular music so representative of capitalist society, and I didn't worry: mentally I kept practicing my own tunes and the lines of my refined songs about psychiatric hospitals, the status of women, and state-approved slaughter.

The uproar did not quiet down even after the singer and her group had disappeared. I looked for the mayor, ready to get up on stage with the confidence of a clear political statement, if not exactly along the Party line.

The mayor took hold of the mike, inviting the crowd to calm down, without too much success. He came down from the stage and pushed around two or three particularly vociferous guys with whom he exchanged obscure words in their dialect. He came close to me. I was ready.

"Listen, maybe it's better that we just move on to the speech right away; I apologize, but you know this is the first time that a woman has sung, and the comrades . . ."

I understood, and all my stage confidence, recently acquired anyway, dissipated. My lips and my legs began to shake as at the times of my first performances; I told the mayor that I could not accept this; and got up on stage. His eyes showed dismay. Pale and tense, he tried to do something to calm down at least those around him: he shoved and elbowed, but it didn't work.

I looked at the square—all those dark heads and no faces—I cleared my voice: it was no longer a question of lozenges; the knot in my throat was fear.

Regretfully, I looked for a moment at the sophisticated pro-gram pasted on my guitar: songs to be sung with a loud voice, important texts filled with consciousness and nuances.

I started singing *Bandiera rossa* (Red Flag) at the top of my lungs. The mayor, still shoving people around, joined me in singing along with the elderly men, who were brought about by the Communist hymn to a nonnegotiable order. Before the song was over the square was already calm; even the young people were singing. For the first time I praised the "revolutionary disci-pline" against which I had fought so many times. The final applause was solid.

I went through the entire repertory of the most popular hymns, and at the end I could afford to sing some of the more involved songs: I carefully avoided all those about women's issues.

After the show, visibly relieved, the mayor took me to city hall and then to various houses: it was difficult and rude to turn down the glass of wine or the greasy fritters. I didn't know how to shield myself. In the end, I was won over by an elderly woman who pre-sented me with an enormous roll filled with sausages and sweet peppers: an obvious combination I had never thought of, a good antidote to the robust wine.

She had a sort of Christmas tree next to her window, a green branch holding the pictures of many deceased people: from Togliatti to Anne Frank, to her sons. And at the top of it, like a guiding star, a title in fading red ink from the Party's paper, *l'Unità*, saying: "The Swindle Law did not pass."

HAMBONE WITH BEANS

1 hambone with some meat still on it, cut into 4 sections
2 cups dry pinto beans
1 large onion
2 T. tomato paste
oil
salt

I drop the bone in boiling water and let it cook for about ten minutes, then I drain it. I repeat this operation three more times, always starting with clean water.

After the onion is lightly sautéed in the oil, I add the beans (which have been soaking for twelve hours) and a quantity of water twice their volume. I cook them about one hour. When the beans are done, I add the tomato paste and the bones and let it all simmer for another half hour.

I generally use very little salt or no salt at all: ham is very salty by itself.

During ten years of working in cinema I had hidden food as an embarrassment. I would eat and cook secretly, only with my closest friends who were not of the "circle"; inside the frivolous, elegant, and educated world to which I felt I should belong, the word "kitchen" did not have citizenship.

Actually, Amidei boasted about his peasant omelet. As part of the History of Cinema he could afford to: he would never have risked having his treated white hair being permeated with the repugnant stench of fried oil. We—the group with which I wanted to identify—were all young, not famous, for one reason or another sort of marginal. New privileged children of the night, we nibbled and tasted food: luxurious breakfasts at irregular hours, never real meals. Anything resembling a complete meal we reserved exclusively for restaurants. We showed no apparent interest in food, all the while talking about other things. On Amidei's terrace, to which I had access as his secretary, I only asked for brand name teas, spiritual and insubstantial.

Those lively and desperate days during the Italian Film Festival: Venice in August, splendid and impossible to work in. Dawns by the canals after entire nights spent with the duplicating machine, one last cigarette with the chemical plant workers, who escorted me to my hotel because of the fascists roaming around.

The grave semi-clandestine arrival of the Soviet delegation, the feast of banned movies on gondolas and yachts, Godard playing chess, the hug from Zavattini, young and sleepless. Mountains and mountains of paper, feeling like a drop in the wide sea.

I wonder how I knew that it would be okay to prepare a bean dish for Massimo. Perhaps it was his frank smile, maybe his sensitive, firm hands. We still had a lot to untangle between us; he wasn't showing signs of wanting to and I couldn't understand whether it was unwillingness or shyness. We had only shared a bottle of red wine and some cheese leftovers.

Having to face hypotheses that were too well-defined, some of us wavered; others withdrew, most fled without excuses. Bitter refusals. Would I ever decide to hold my tongue, pretending to let myself be seduced? I tried, I invited about ten people from the outer circle: I had three hambones, big pots, a day of hard work and apprehension.

Supper went smoothly between anecdotes about cinema, Socialist songs, Spartacus Picenus' songs, an ironic and sorrowful self-display. I showed myself to be an adequate mistress of the house; tension kept me away from Massimo. It was his birthday, the film critic alluded to my past loves, the assistant director of the film festival was distant, amiable, and civil: stiffly, in a corner of the hall, I gave Massimo a birthday card. It doesn't matter if it is already over—I told myself—it's a relationship like many others.

They all left, Massimo disappeared last around the curve of the staircases, without a gesture or a look. I cleared off the table slowly, carefully, allowing time for his possible return, a phone call.

I decided to go to sleep, and was almost calm. I had made a mistake again, nothing new there. My past experiences would come to my aid; I was already feeling sleepy.

When the bell rang, I was almost falling asleep. It was the beginning of a relationship that was not like the others.

PORK CHOPS WITH ORANGES

4 pork chops
4 oranges
salt

I squeeze two oranges. I peel and thinly slice the other two. I tie the four chops together, alternating with the orange slices. I place them in a deep baking dish together with the juice and the rest of the slices, then I salt them and bake them for forty-five minutes, turning them from time to time. If the sauce looks too thin, I reduce it rapidly on the stove.

The group was coming apart, we argued about everything: which movie to see and whether to go to see it together, plans for an afternoon excursion, how to raise children.

That particular time it was about the New Year's Day menu. Still obstinately together, we allowed ourselves to be carried away by practical issues. It seemed indispensable not only that we all spend exactly the same amount of money, but also the same amount of time in the kitchen, making sure that the results were not going to favor somebody's culinary abilities at the expense of another's.

But because it was New Year's Day, we also expected to eat well and enjoy ourselves.

Fascinating, restless, distant, Fosco was observing us from a corner of the room, unavoidably aristocratic even in his jeans and army shirt, pain sculpted in his hollow face. His expression showed the nonpatronizing disenchantment of someone who had already lived a similar experience and was now involved in more serious things.

We were discussing food, the ever-present ghosts of other things always behind and inside us.

Fosco was waiting for some of us to leave to begin talking about himself, and anyhow, he was getting bored. He proposed his mother's pork chops with oranges; it was inexpensive and required little cooking time.

The king was naked: we accepted his directions. It was the last New Year's Day we spent together.

CREPES

2 cups flour
3 eggs
2 T. oil
2 cups milk
salt

I beat the eggs lightly, then gradually add the flour. I continue to stir until it is well blended. I then add the oil, salt, and then, gradually, the milk.

If possible I let the mixture rest for a couple of hours, but this is not absolutely necessary.

Since I have acquired a crepe pan the process has been much simpler and more foolproof, but even with a frying pan, it was not very difficult. The important thing (and this can only be learned by practicing) is to grease the pan just the right amount (crepes must not be *fried*) and to put the right amount of mixture in the pan (a minimal amount, so that when I tilt the pan the bottom will be covered by a very thin layer).

It is enough (in fact, I believe it is better) to cook the crepes only on one side, without flipping them over: this way they will stay softer.

The recipes for the filling are practically infinite; those that I use most often are:

MUSHROOM CREPES

4 T. butter
2 T. flour

2 cups milk

3 T. grated Parmesan

1/3 oz. dried porcini mushrooms

nutmeg

salt

I soak the mushrooms in an inch or so of warm milk. Meanwhile, I prepare a béchamel with the other ingredients. When it is almost ready, I add the mushrooms and let it all cook another few minutes.

I fill the crepes and arrange them in an ovenproof baking dish, and then I dot them with butter. Immediately before serving, I warm them in the oven for a few minutes.

RICOTTA CREPES

8 oz. ricotta

2 T. milk

2 T. Parmesan cheese

2 T. chopped parsley

I mix all the ingredients thoroughly, then I spread the mixture on the crepes and roll them up like a strudel.

CREAM OF CHICKEN CREPES

1 chicken breast

butter

salt

3 T. béchamel

I cook the chicken breast in the butter; I put it through the food mill, and mix it into the béchamel. I then spread it on the crepes, which I then roll up cigarette-like, dot with butter and warm for a few minutes in the oven before serving.

CREPES WITH FINANZIERA SAUCE

1 1/4 lb. spinach

butter

salt
A good meat sauce, with chicken livers, etc.

I cook the spinach with no water and with a pinch of salt in a covered pan on low heat. After five minutes, I remove it from the burner and chop it, then I return it to the burner for a few seconds with a good amount of melted butter. I fill the crepes with spinach (they must be quite full), and serve them with the piping hot *finanziera*, which is a particularly rich meat sauce.

One day, when I was fourteen, as I was coming home from school I decided to leave home. Not *run away*: I had acquired a certain taste, a sense of irony that at times was able to keep me away from melodrama.

I called my sister Ada, and moved in with her: my father and mother were duly informed, in the spirit of revenge that characterized Ada's relationship with her stepmother, who was one year younger than she.

Seventeen years older than I, Ada was elegance, freedom, risk, imagination: everything that in my own home seemed frozen in rigid and foreign rules.

I knew that she was pregnant when she married, that she had crossed the Iron Curtain without a passport in order to follow her husband, and that when she argued with Father they spoke French. She had come back to Italy with two children and no husband. Now she was an interpreter; she traveled around the world and had a new man, Sergio, the only liberal figure who had ever appeared on the family scene.

Liters of perfume, stylish clothes, Ada was the only person in the family or among my acquaintances who dyed her hair (she said that our mother had done it too, but all about our mother and her experiences belonged to her and not to me). She taught me to use rouge and foundation, when just a touch of eyeliner was worth all my father's ranting and raving (his prediction was always the same: "you are going to end up a streetwalker under the portico of Piazza Vittorio").

The month that I spent in her house was a long breath of fresh air, a frenzied enjoyment of everything that in my home was forbidden. Sergio spoke of sexuality as something that could concern me too, and Ada gave me the nylons that I had wanted so much I could not sleep at night. I could read Lawrence without hiding.

In the house there was the smell of luxury and indulgence that I had longed for, and would still for a long time. They drank whiskey, and ate prosciutto from Parma. Who would ever have thought, in my house, to add cream to the pasta, or Marsala to that detested staple, the pan-fried cutlet? With Ada these miracles were possible every day, and for special occasions (which were often: it was enough to just feel like it) there were crepes, both as main dishes and desserts.

Toward the end of the month an aunt arrived from Israel. She gave me a lecture, and spoke of the right relationships that there must be between a daughter and her parents. I listened with a growing sense of irritation. I said that I had no complaint about my mother, but that life with my father was becoming unbearable. Ada looked at me and for the moment didn't speak, but when we were alone she said I should never forget that my father really was my father, and the woman I called mommy was only a stepmother.

With a sense of desperation I defended my position; Ada was asking me to keep my feet in stirrups that were lacerating me.

The little "bond of kisses" that had joined us together broke then: mending it was never again possible.

ONION OMELET

4 medium onions
4 eggs
a few drops of lemon juice
oil
salt

I slice the onions thinly and sauté them in the oil and lemon juice. They must be cooked patiently on low heat until they become golden but not fried or burned. I remove the omelet before it is fully cooked, to keep it tender and runny.

NETTLE OMELET

1 bunch nettles
4 eggs

1 T. grated Parmesan
butter
salt

I cook the tender and whole nettle leaves in a small amount of boiling salted water. I drain them and squeeze the water out, and then I soften them in the butter. I then add the beaten eggs with the salt and the Parmesan. I remove the omelet from the heat when it is still quite tender.

OMELET WITH BOCCONCINI

4 eggs
2 soft herb cheeses (or 2 T. grated Parmesan and a few
   chopped basil leaves)
1 hard roll, diced
butter
salt

I sauté the diced bread, and add the eggs beaten with the cheese.

It has often happened to me to travel through the world unaware, encased in an outer shell of impermeability. This reached its acme, I believe, between 1968 and 1969. Involved as I was with matters of survival (among others), events passed before my eyes without my being able to grasp their significance. I bought the newspaper every day, I read Marcuse, and remained irremediably on the outside, so much as to be still convinced of my status not only as emancipated, but as a "new" woman.

In 1969, in December, I cut a record—the only one of my singing career—which was so bad it never came out. On my way to the recording studio the bus passed through a metalworkers' demonstration. I hugged my guitar, my eyes low.

For the choruses, Giovanni, an eighteen-year-old with a bright future who intrigued me, joined me at the microphone. We teased each other; there were games between us that were not innocent ones, and taboos that were difficult to break. On the way home together we passed the demonstration again. His was already another generation, and his eyes saw different things than those that I was thinking.

On the stairs we spoke of Rossanda and Pintor,[1] and in the house we felt hungry. Not much in the refrigerator, as usual.

I began sautéeing some stale bread that burned a little, and the eggs were not too fresh. The taboos required that I play out a maternal role ("eat up so you'll grow big and strong"). The not-so-innocent games tightened my stomach, but he handled them with much greater aplomb.

After dinner we practiced the choruses, then I tried to make my strong, loud voice follow his cruel and absentminded tales.

Before midnight he left with a brief ambiguous embrace; he didn't yet have his driver's license and could not miss the last bus.

(The night he finished recording his first album be phoned me, and his voice was no longer that of a boy. Who knows if he realized it, but I knew he had decided.)

Such an embarrassment when he arrived at my house. I had company, and Massimo was there. I had to choose, and I chose Massimo. Giovanni sang for everyone, irritable and a little drunk. I haven't seen him since. I had chosen the life as a couple, and everything else has faded, lost along the way without apparent pain.

EGG FETTUCCINE

4 eggs
1 T. flour
2 T. milk
4 "Roma" tomatoes
2 T. Parmesan cheese
1 clove garlic
8 basil leaves
oil
salt

I mix eggs, flour, milk and salt, and prepare several very thin omelets that I cut into strips and arrange in a shallow dish. Right before serving I pour a sauce over them, which I make in the following manner: I sauté the garlic, add the tomatoes, chopped in the blender or passed through a large-holed sieve, and I thicken it for a few seconds on a high flame. I top it with Parmesan cheese and chopped basil and serve immediately.

CHILDREN'S OMELET

4 eggs
4 T. Parmesan
4 basil leaves, chopped
1/2 cup milk
salt

I beat all the ingredients together, and place them in the oven in a nonstick baking dish for about fifteen minutes at 430^0 degrees.

ZUCCHINI OMELET

4 zucchini
4 eggs
oil
salt

I slice the zucchini thinly and sauté them, then add the eggs. It is much better if eaten cold.

My father had the Formia house built right after the war using scrap materials in order to save money. It was meant to be a *pied-á-terre* between Rome and Naples or Portici to be more exact, his chosen home and electoral constituency.

For the first three years, I went there with my mother: our bathing suits were woolen and high cut, and we had to change immediately after bathing to avoid blisters and redness. The flies were relentless, and bug spray kept the mosquitoes away only for a short time. The only mementos are a few photos of a lady in an attractive scoop-necked dress, next to a bright-eyed little girl. Her letters say that hiding for a few moments in the shadow of the bathhouses was enough for me to immediately come down with a fever.

I returned to Formia with Giulia and Ada and her children Federico and Katinka, raised in a Czechoslovakian nursery.

Ada was preparing for the entrance exam for Interpreters' School, and from the record player there came the sounds of French existentialism.

Giulia had low-cut dresses, and Ada had a red underskirt with black lace, bought at the American market. When they went dancing at "Le Palme" in the evening I babysat my niece and nephew, who never called me aunt because of the small age difference. My sisters had friends who wore white Navy uniforms and who sailed on the ocean liner *Amerigo Vespucci*. As I sat by the edge of the road carefully dusting the sand off my feet before leaving, I could catch a glimpse of their courtship between the beach cabins.

The house was far from the sea, in the hills; from the terrace one could see a large piece of the gulf, and the mountains began from the little uphill road right behind us. Later they started a bus service, and we would get off at the beach with Katinka in her carriage. On the way back the sun beat on the steep uphill road. Under the bridge over the Appian Way was a donkey's carcass.

Soon I stopped going to the beach. I preferred to remain mistress of the house that opened onto the garden. At times I would wash the windows—no one asked me to, but I liked the clean freshness emerging from the newspaper that I used. Toward fall I would have liked to turn on the terracotta stove, but I was told that the birds that had nested in the chimney would die. Other times I would read. I had gone through all the children's books, and my father gave me inexpensive editions of Russian classics and the Stalin Prize winners, big red volumes full of dark stories and tortures, in which everyone died or went mad or became invalid. A friend lent me the *Delly* series. I read it and was engrossed by it, but felt it my duty to relegate it among the inanities.

My chore was to buy the bread from Gaetano's fly-filled shop, inside the guard tower called Castellone. Ada would cut large slices (the butter in the icebox was never really hard) and we would eat sitting in a semicircle on tree-trunk seats in front of the glass doors so as not to drop crumbs inside the house.

In the vegetable garden there were black figs, tomatoes, lemons, a few strawberries, the climbing squash planted by my mother before her death, and a few vegetables. We would eat in an uncivilized manner; I didn't constantly have someone after me to check on how I ate and how much. Ada, it was clear, was filled with *joie de vivre*, and on special days she would make Neapolitan pizza and salty fried rounds made of leavened dough.

Father and mother came every now and then, tired and hot, in the imposing Fiat "1400," which was put to the test every time on the dusty curves of the Appian Way. (When we traveled together, we would stop at Itri, and my father would tell the story of *Fra'Diavolo*, and would sing the aria *Quell'uom dal fiero aspetto.*)

They did not stay long, the sea either was bad for my father or it bored him. They stayed just long enough for a zucchini omelet, a ritual preserved even in the prison years, and which Ada kept up religiously, careful to remain the priestess of a family life that I had never known.

During the longer stays my father would go down to the sea around sunset for a walk on the beach. He would go along the shoreline with his hands clasped behind his back, his torso white, his legs thin inside his shorts. Sometimes I went with him.

Pietro Nenni wore a beret even on the beach; his villa was right by the shore. Remigio Paone, on the other hand, had a bungalow in the middle of the water, and it could be accessed by means of a walkway on stilts. All around there were rowboats and even motorboats. There were rumored to be elegant parties, but it was the statesman's isolation that was most known and felt. A hazy memory, maybe not even true: the politicians are walking side by side, hands behind their backs like old prisoners. Nenni gave me a sense of friendship. I stayed behind to gather seashells. Who knows what their words were, covered by the noise of the sea. The People's Front was already a spent experience; perhaps stiff, so-called informal negotiations, perhaps the shared pain that came from women they loved, or from friends killed in the war.

Then my father and his wife would leave, toward an exclusive world enclosed within a single key word: the *Party*. I would wave to them from the gate, or from among the branches of the bougainvillea. She would leave me a little frivolous gift; my father would leave me books and advice. The house once again became empty, and mine.

For many years I did not know where the mountain road lead, beyond the dusty curve. In my dreams there was a big field of beautiful yellow flowers; it was a cemetery. I was disappointed when I found vegetable gardens, vineyards, and the bare expanses that lead to Santa Maria della Noce.

6

Vegetables

LETTUCE WITH PESTO

1 head of lettuce
1 garlic clove
6 basil leaves
2 T. oil
salt

I mince the garlic and the basil finely and place the mixture in a bowl; I slowly incorporate the oil (as when making mayonnaise). I let the mixture stand for a few hours. About a half hour before serving, I dress the salad with it.

When we lived in the house on Viale XXI Aprile, to me salad meant the small lettuce heart, the king's morsel, awarded to me, if not exactly as a sign of preference, at least as one of distinction.

Around the Torre Gaia house there were fields and fields of lettuce. My father praised the joys of country life: he seemed serene and more alone. My sister Stefania was born right after we moved there. Deposed from my throne, I would eat the salad only if forced.

For my first house with its enormous terrace, I hauled potting vases from windowsills and entrance halls of well-to-do homes. My sister Ada gave me a red geranium, which in spring burst with flowers and with basil from a prior, forgotten sowing.

I didn't own a stove yet, so salads were my only option. But I didn't mind them anymore, as they were the staple of each meal. The basil (oh, the scent it spread at night when I watered it!) picked right before serving, became an integral part of my salads, one of my trademarks: something extra, an aroma, a detail. Thereafter, never, in all the houses where I have lived, have I done without a pot of basil on my windowsill.

ORANGE AND FENNEL SALAD

2 fennel bulbs
2 oranges
8 Greek olives
oil
vinegar
salt

I find peeling oranges very boring, especially when I need a lot of them. A system to simplify the operation is to put them in a hot oven for two or three minutes: the peel comes off much more easily, even the inside skin.

So, I peel the oranges and cut them into small chunks, and do the same with the fennel. I add the olives and dress the salad, but not at the last minute.

SPINACH SALAD

1/2 lb. raw spinach
1 oz. prosciutto
1/2 lemon
oil
a pinch of salt

I wash the spinach, which must be small and tender; I shred the prosciutto into small pieces and sauté it in a little oil (as I do to prepare the *carbonara*), then I pour all this, while still hot, onto the coarsely-shredded spinach. To finish I add lemon juice, and salt if necessary.

MUSHROOM SALAD

3/4 lb. mushrooms
juice of 1 lemon
1 garlic clove, minced

1 T. minced parsley

oil

salt

I slice the mushrooms very finely and set them aside for half an hour. Then I combine them with all the other ingredients. Sometimes I also add a few shavings of Parmesan cheese.

After months of silence, Aldo telephoned to invite us to his housewarming; reading between the lines, one could assume that he was going to introduce us to a new woman in his life. We had not seen each other for a long time: from the ashes of the group, each one had gone on his or her own way, all of us more alone, all determined to not repeat the same mistakes.

I had seen Aldo at my father's funeral: he had come for my sake, certainly not to honor the Party leader. Yet he did not greet me, he stayed visible enough and distant within the crowd.

His invitation did not appeal to me; I didn't want to leave Tommaso, who was a few months old, and I didn't want to see Aldo or the others; the wounds were still painful.

Aldo's house was normal, clean, perhaps exceedingly in order; so different from the monastic and slovenly simplicity I had known him for. The revolutionary literature was locked inside cabinets that made it invisible.

In the kitchen, Aldo's woman, intimidated by the presence of people who she knew were important to him, was preparing delicacies. I went to help her; she was dressed tastefully, her hair fresh from the beauty parlor. She was my age; many things made us similar and close.

Aldo was shuttling between the kitchen and the living room, thoughtful and a bit anxious with everybody. He stirred a pot and I saw the color of his face change: a large piece of hot pepper was swimming in the pot, and he remembered my allergy.

I demurred, saying that it wasn't important, that he shouldn't worry. The abundant presence of hot pepper in all the dishes scared me, I knew how dearly I would pay for it, but I did not want to disappoint Aldo once more. His woman improvised with a mushroom salad, and he dressed it and put it aside for me.

APPLE SALAD

1 Granny Smith apple
1 orange
2 heads of Belgian lettuce
6 Greek olives
oil
vinegar
salt
soy sauce

There is only one way to adjust ingredients: taste, taste, taste.

NETTLE BALLS

2 lbs. nettles
3 eggs
2 T. flour
2 T. grated Parmesan cheese
oil
salt
cooking juices from a roast

I boil the nettles in a little water, squeeze them, and chop them. I add the beaten eggs, flour, Parmesan cheese, salt. I make small patties that I fry in abundant oil and then simmer briefly in the cooking juice from the roast.

Since it rarely happens now that I go for a stroll and pick nettles, I often replace them with spinach.

BOILED ARTICHOCKES

Boiled artichokes are no longer popular, but as a child there were special plates to serve them, with a small cavity in the middle, to hold the dip.

I did not like the soft, hairy heart (all children hate that part), but my father insisted on its superiority.

How much bread dipped in oil I ate just to swallow the small pieces of artichoke heart!

SKILLET ENDIVE

1 lb. endive
2 large onions
oil
salt

I sauté the onions in a skillet large enough to fit the endive, which is very voluminous. When the onions start to turn gold, I add the endive and the salt, cover with the lid, and let it simmer slowly for about twenty minutes.

PICKLED EGGPLANTS

eggplants
vegetable oil
vinegar
garlic
parsley
basil
salt

I slice the eggplant lengthwise half an inch thick and criss-cross the tops with a knife. I place the slices in a baking dish with plenty of oil and bake for about twenty minutes at 450° F. A single baking dish may not be enough, the slices take lots of space. In this case, I recycle the same oil for the following baking, adding a little more each time.

I drain the slices well, dry them on brown paper, and arrange them in layers in a container, sprinkling salt in between. Meanwhile, I warm up a little vinegar with minced garlic, parsley, and basil leaves. I pour all this on the eggplant, which must marinate for a couple of hours at least.

Unlike other vegetables, which become mushy and inedible, these eggplants keep very well in the freezer. That is a reason I always make a lot of them each time.

BAKED EGGPLANTS IN WHITE SAUCE

2 lbs. eggplant
1/4 cup butter

2 T. flour
2 cups milk
4 oz. sharp Provolone cheese
4 oz. fontina cheese
4 oz. Gruyère cheese
4 oz. grated Parmesan cheese
a pinch of nutmeg
salt

Using plenty of oil, I fry the eggplant cut lengthwise in thin slices. Meanwhile, I prepare the béchamel sauce with the butter, flour, milk, nutmeg, salt. (Every cookbook has a recipe for béchamel sauce: but not one of them mentions that flour and butter must brown together at least five minutes before adding the milk.) When the béchamel is ready, I add the cheeses, diced, and the Parmesan, and let them melt a bit.

I pour a layer of this mixture on the bottom of a baking dish, then a layer of eggplant, well drained of the oil. I alternate layers and sauce, ending with the béchamel, and bake in a hot oven for a few minutes, until it forms a brown crust.

For Massimo's birthday, which was also our first anniversary, the group was solidly united, still capable of attracting a number of other people in its orbit.

The eggplant had to be enough for thirty or more friends. I prepared the béchamel with the cheeses, and each woman of the group brought two pounds of eggplant already fried. We ended up with fourteen pounds of them, some white, some purple. The baking dishes flying in and out of the oven were forging relationships formed around our being together, and blending our differences.

Late into the night, we sang protest songs, songs of the struggle: in 1975 everything was still clear and within our reach.

SAVOY CABBAGE AND ONIONS

1 lb. cabbage
1 lb. onions
oil
salt

On the cutting board, I cut the cabbage into thin strips. I sauté the onions, coarsely chopped, and then add the cabbage and salt. I let it cook over medium heat, covered, for about twenty minutes.

The obstetrician read the results of my glucose test and his lips contracted slightly.

"Can your regular doctor prescribe you a diet?" he asked me.

My doctor had not noticed any abnormality in the tests.

"Probably not," I answered.

He then said that the best thing for me to do was to spend two or three days in the Gemelli Hospital: they would do the necessary tests, and thus prescribe a suitable diet and set the insulin dosage.

Massimo took me to the hospital in the early afternoon; the initial formalities took until dark, and I arrived in the assigned ward around seven.

The main lights were already turned off; the women, all in bed and immobilized by the IVs, seemed to be asleep. A doctor came to ask me a number of questions: they brought me food to eat although it was past the time. Eyes were looking at me from the nearby beds. I was put on an IV as well. I asked the nurse for explanations but she only said that those were her orders. Before turning off my light, I applied antistretch cream to my stomach as I did every night: from the nearby beds came mean and derisive glances. A voice commented, without addressing me, that it was all useless. And as if to prove it, the bed next to me exposed an enormous young stomach covered with purple streaks that resembled a dartboard.

I didn't sleep that night, more because of the IV than nervousness: I was certain I would have only two or three days of hospital stay. I asked the obstetrician in the morning while she was examining me. From the other beds came smirks and more looks.

With great surprise I observed the women moving from bed to bed hauling their IV trees behind them. They washed themselves, they knitted: I stood there motionless, my arm disabled and tingling. I tried to read: it seemed to be the only possible activity in those conditions.

During the following days, amid tests, and examinations, I began to understand that I would not get out of there until after delivery, like those women who had been there for three, for five, some for eight months. None of them were talking to me: they were talking, often heatedly, among themselves and they made fun of my book, my newspaper, my antistretch cream.

I had to survive, so I put away my reading and tried in any way I could to initiate small talk. But it was no use; their rage kept me away from them. I was different because I received visits from people every day, while they only had relatives from the South coming to see them every two weeks.

I got used to the IV and discovered I could do a lot of things in spite of it. I had knitting needles and wool brought to me, and I started to make a little red sweater for that child who I was gradually beginning to see as both threatened and threatening.

My open-stitch baby sweater came out soft and delicate; the sweaters produced by their hands were meant to last a lifetime. While I was putting it together the woman who was most hostile (she had been in the hospital for seven months; she took insulin even at night and then proceeded to gulp down a huge roll and a large cup of milk) came close to me and said: "Now you show me how you do it."

I had been admitted. I entered into the depth of the logic of the institution: the outside world was an unbearable thought, the only safety net was to focus oneself exclusively on that inside made of amniocentesis, monitoring, glucose readings. We compared data as though it were a Cabal, mysterious signs that bound us together. Only our fear was not shared or communicated.

At last I was accepted, even though they continued to view my diet with suspicion since I strictly followed the doctor's instructions, which was the reason I was there. The women had told me:

"Don't worry, we'll take care of you. These people are going let you die."

In the gestational pathology's ward, where the best of cases had diabetes, nobody followed the prescribed diet. The scientifically-measured hospital food was looked down upon with revulsion, barely tasted, and when the head nurse left, the real meal appeared: jars filled with sausages in oil, dried fruit, desserts, chocolate.

I didn't find it too hard to resist the temptations, except when I saw in front of me a container full of cabbage swimming in oil, the scent of onions permeating the ward. I ate my plain hospital vegetables courageously, feeling very brave and very stupid, amid a feast of cabbage and *taralli* (ring-shaped biscuits) from Puglia.

And to this day I ask myself: what if I had eaten them? How serious would it have been?

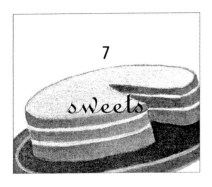

7

sweets

SEMOLINA PUDDING

1 qt. milk
5 oz. semolina
3 egg yolks
4 T. sugar, plus an additional 6 T. for the caramel sauce
1 T. rum
1 handful raisins
1 T. butter
rind of 2 lemons

I heat the milk along with the lemon rinds and sugar, and when it comes to a boil I sprinkle in the semolina and stir as it cooks, for about ten minutes. I remove it from the heat, then in a pudding mold I caramelize the sugar, adding a demitasse of water when it is quite dark, so that it will dissolve better. To the semolina I add the raisins, softened in warm water and well drained, the butter, and the rum. Finally I add the egg yolks, stirring quickly so they will not cook. I pour the mixture into the mold, and place it in a warm oven (about 300⁰ F.) for about fifteen minutes, then put it in the refrigerator to chill.

For years I believed that Grandmother Alfonsa's semolina pudding was the ultimate treat for every child, as it had been for me. Tommaso never wanted to try it.

I am told that to make him like it I ought to sprinkle it with chocolate: too radical a transformation, one for which I am not yet prepared.

APPLE CAKE

2 1/4 cups flour
12 T. butter or margarine
6 oz. sugar
3 eggs
4 delicious apples
1 handful raisins
2 shot glasses rum
2 t. baking powder

I soak the apples, thinly sliced, in the rum and sugar. Meanwhile I beat the eggs, add the flour, the butter, melted and cooled, and the raisins. I add the apples, sugar, rum, and mix well again. Finally I add the baking powder.

I pour the mixture in a buttered and floured cake pan with fairly high sides to allow the cake to rise, then place it into the oven at 430° F. for forty-five minutes.

To really go all out (which I sometimes do) one can serve the cake with heavy cream to be poured and spread individually over each slice.

At last Aldo too is going to have a child. In the midst of doubts and crises, he too has accepted the fact that all one can do is live. He has even accepted me.

His partner continues to cook in grand style. By now we have gotten to know each other and she spares me the hot peppers: we know almost everything about each other's intolerances and have learned to be careful. We all sometimes feel a bit distanced from each other now, feeling the regret of that wholeness that we never achieved, and the loss of an exuberance that fleetingly touched us and was gone. We don't even talk about it anymore; hurt upon hurt we have learned that in the formula for survival, restraint is an essential element.

For a dinner together she asks me to contribute a dessert without milk. Once viewed as the supreme antidote, milk has been transformed into a dark evil, one of the many unexploded mines that threaten the unborn child.

I could simply make a jam tart; instead I make up an apple cake, putting my creativity—and the ingredients I have around the house—at the service of an unfathomable future of children yet to be born, loved, protected. I, however, can no longer pretend to share in that experience.

CHOCOLATE MOUSSE

4 very fresh eggs
4 1/2 oz. dark chocolate
3 t. strong coffee
3/4 cup whipping cream

I break up the chocolate into bits, melt it in a double boiler along with the coffee, pour it into a mixing bowl, and let it cool. I combine the egg yolks and mix well, then, stirring carefully I add the egg whites, which I have beaten until very stiff. Finally, I add a tablespoon of the cream, which meanwhile I have whipped; the rest is for decorating.

I let the mousse set in the refrigerator for at least twenty-four hours to allow it to thicken and set properly.

The mousse is Ada: France, charm. Hers always turn out perfectly, mine almost never do. So I use it not so much by itself as I do to fill cakes: especially for Tommaso's parties.

The first time I made it I was shaking, taking a risk with a cake that was not store-bought. Children can be so uncompromising.

The party was in Via Forlí with everyone standing up and singing *Caterina* like a hymn, and the children asking how our son came to be born. Tommaso was tense, the center of attention.

They were stuffing themselves with little pizzas and Cokes; would there be any room left for the cake? Tommaso blew out the candles, received his applause, and ran outside to get a handle on his excitement. He came back in and watched out of the corner of his eye to see how it would turn out.

I was slicing the cake, and the children, sitting in a circle, stared for a long time before taking a bite.

Carlo, solitary and testy leader, gave the go-ahead.

He said:

"It's good, mamma Clara. Don't you find it a little similar to *tegolino*[1]?"

And even Tommaso ate it.

CHRISTMAS CAKE

4 cups flour

3 eggs

1 1/2 cubes of yeast

10 oz. sugar

2 t. vanilla

4 oz. margarine

5 lb. canned fruit (or pears and apples cooked in 2 cups
  sweet wine)

2 oranges

rind of 2 lemons

6 oz. dried figs

8 oz. walnuts

10 oz. raisins

8 oz. almonds

6 oz. hazelnuts

1 envelope baking powder

I knead together flour, sugar, vanilla, the cubes of yeast dissolved in warm water, a pinch of salt, and part of the liquid from the fruit, until I have a rather solid dough which I let rise for four hours. Meanwhile, I heat the fruit with the remaining liquid, along with the oranges cut into thin slices, the lemon peel cut into thin strips, and the margarine. When the mixture is quite hot, I add the raisins, which have been softened in water and drained, and the figs, cut into bits. I mix well and add all the nuts.

I transfer the leavened dough to a large bowl and mix in first the eggs, beaten, then the fruit mixture, using a long handled wooden spoon kept for this particular task. I obtain a rather liquid dough, into which I finally mix the baking powder.

For baking, I use loaf pans, which I grease, flour, and fill three-quarters of the way. I place the baking pans in a preheated oven (480° F.), which I lower to 430° F. after about ten minutes, and bake for one hour.

When they are cooled, I remove the cakes from the pans, brush the tops with a water and sugar glaze, and let them set (for up to a few days) on brown paper, to allow them to dry thoroughly.

There have been years in which, living away from home, I thought that a regrouping among us would be possible, was indeed already taking place. That is when this cake began: a labor-intensive cake, as one can see. It's necessary to plan ahead during the summer to prepare the fruit; then, an entire afternoon with my mother, Stefania, and Micol to shell the nuts and to play kitchen. Finally there were the baking pans and molds, the smell of Christmas around the house, lots of sweets to eat and to give: the amounts we made were three times this one.

Then many assumptions collapsed, there were moments in which the Christmas cake seemed intolerable; the burden of a ritual from which we could not extricate ourselves was weighted down by a real lack of communication.

Gestures that have been repeated over the years: the amounts become smaller, but in the summer I still prepare the fruit.

ALLORINI

4 oz. honey
4 oz. chopped hazelnuts or almonds
30 laurel (bay) leaves

I heat the honey on a low flame, add the nuts, and cook for twenty minutes, while stirring.

I pour the mixture onto an oiled tabletop, spread it with the blade of a knife to a thickness of 1/4 inch. Before it cools I score the mixture in a criss-cross pattern, to form diamond shapes with sides about 1 1/2 inches long.

When the mixture is completely cool, I break the diamonds apart and sandwich them between the bay leaves, piling them to keep them closed.

After a few days they may be eaten or given as gifts.

ZABAIONE ICE CREAM

7 egg yolks
7 T. dry Marsala wine
7 T. sugar
2 cups heavy cream
10 almonds
1/2 oz. dark chocolate

I beat the egg yolks, sugar, and Marsala together and cook the *zabaione* in a double boiler for twenty minutes, stirring constantly with a wooden spoon.

I allow the *zabaione* to cool, and meanwhile I prepare the following: the almonds, which I chop coarsely and toast two or three minutes in a warm oven, and the cream, which I whip thoroughly. I then gradually fold the *zabaione* into the whipped cream.

I place half the mixture in a container in the freezer and let it chill for a half hour, after which I cover the surface, which should already be hardened, with the almonds and chocolate shavings. I then spread the remaining mixture on the top and put it back in the freezer. If properly stored, this ice cream keeps for a rather long time; therefore I can prepare it well in advance of the time I plan to use it. All I need to do is put it in the refrigerator an hour before it is to be eaten.

The scent of riches and luxury that as a child I longed for in the silver and in the Yom Kippur olives is one of the "red threads" of my life. In 1968 I professed my love for beautiful things, albeit in the knowledge that I would not have sold my soul to obtain them. Then, for increasingly practical reasons, the beautiful things almost disappeared from my life, absorbed by other choices and other expenses without ceasing, however, to be an undercurrent. It is what has made me reject, with growing intolerance, the latest fashions and the best-sellers, that which—after the obligatory phases of complete forswearing—brings me to choose linens and perfumes over dresses, that which inspires me to give eternal gratitude, if not love, to anyone who gives me a rose. (Few people have the ability to give me gifts: the thin skin that I always think I show the world apparently comes across like a hard shell that prevents others, and me, from shows of emotion and affection.)

But the red thread does not mean absolute clarity, much less confidence: proof of this rests in my constant pursuit (which comes from an implicit sense of inferiority) of a scent of conspicuous riches through my work, first in filmmaking, then in political conventions.

A similar mechanism operates both in the film world and in the organizational area of political conventions: one works frantically toward the preparation of an *event*, something, which is pure form, and burns out in a very brief time. Meanwhile, everyone can feign equality, the director and the electrician, the politician and the stenographer. The goal seems to be a common one, and the first-name basis gives the illusion of comradeship. A great deal of money circulates, one can feel it in the air, and all that's missing, it seems, is the time to gather it up.

In the world of cinema, culture makes a fleeting appearance (often only sensed, illusory); from the realm of the political conventions it is rigorously excluded. History is reduced to human interest, if not to gossip. The great intrigues of international politics are resolved exclusively in the seating arrangements at a formal banquet, or in the languages chosen for simultaneous translation.

To organize conventions one needs creativity, imagination, impudence; consequently there are mostly women in the profession, excellent heads of household who have gone to the best boarding schools and dress in designer clothes. They are married to the right man (even when they have divorced him), they have known this person and that from the time they were children. They are hard and aggressive businesswomen, often shut inside an unhappiness that they cannot talk about. What weighs on me is the impossibility of building a relationship with them, and at the same time the constant sense of inadequacy that I have inside me. I detest women who live to please, but this does not mean that I have resolved my own conflicts.

I worked at my first convention when I was fourteen. It was for the Green Plan of the Food and Agriculture Organization of

the United Nations: my father was a speaker, Ada was an interpreter, Giulia worked at registration, and I taped the sessions. A
very tall and very black man came up to me at the end of a round
table discussion; I blushed with shyness and from his flow of
words I was only able to grasp "... *enfant* ... *enfant*. ..." He
shook my hand, and I managed a smile, afraid he might kiss me.

Later I found out that he was Senghor; he had met me when
I was a child in my father's arms.

When I then found myself organizing conventions profession-
ally, for days and days, and months and months, I tried to join
that work together with my life, an attempt to grasp, beyond that
polished and scented exterior, a true rapport with some of the
professional women.

The home to which they invited me was—naturally—luxurious: silks, velvets, the old governess in the kitchen, the Filipino
maid that waited on guests. The scent of industry, of chairman-
ship of the board, of banks, fashion, money, wafted in the air.
With a certain desperate look deep in their eyes, sons and daughters of career women showed off the beauty that money can buy,
and their own shallowness. Drugs were not yet a troublesome
presence. The beans they served struck me as unbearable preten-
tiousness.

In the bathroom with the too-ornate faucets I studied the
thickness of the terry-cloth towels, I sampled one of the innumerable bottles of perfume, I sniffed soaps and bubble bath. But it
was all so cold: those things were there to build status: not even
one label that was not famous and expensive. No pleasure, no
connection with the hand-embroidered potpourri sachets that
invade my drawers and scent my life.

The fruit pyramid that dominated the middle of the table was
dismantled under the guests' hands; while the maid served the ice
cream the champagne corks popped. It was a celebration, I
believe, for the second or third billion in earnings.

I searched for some kind of connection in the kitchen; the governess was very flattered when I asked her for the ice cream recipe
and a bit shocked when she learned that I would make it with my
own hands.

CASSATA

1 sponge cake about 1 1/2 lbs.

24 oz. ricotta

4 oz. dark chocolate

1 shot glass sweet liqueur (milk elixir)

1 handful candied fruit

2 or 3 T. sugar

2 cups whipped cream

With a hand mixer (or by passing it through a small-holed sieve) the ricotta should be made smooth and creamy. I mix in the sugar dissolved in a little milk, adding then the candied fruit, finely chopped, and the shaved chocolate.

I cut the cake into very thin slices: it doesn't matter if they break a bit, because I can piece them back together with my hands.

I lay out a first layer of cake and wet it with the liqueur, which I have watered down with an equal amount of water or—even better—of milk. Over the cake I then spread a layer of the ricotta mixture, then more cake with liqueur, and repeat the process ending with a layer of cake (for the top layer I always save the largest and most regular slices). I leave it in the refrigerator for half a day, then I cover it with whipped cream.

When it came time to live together we discussed the matter for months.

Massimo rejected rituals; I wanted us to get married. I still viewed a couple as a transitional entity, a nonpermanent one, destined sooner or later to break up; the idea of having a child never crossed my mind. But I wanted a ceremony, the first one in a life without a first communion or a batmitzvah, almost without gifts at half-hearted birthday celebrations, without a moment in which one feels at the center of the world.

We argued. I reproached Massimo for his childhood filled with affection and things, and received in return his confessions, sometimes bitter, of his fears of being stifled.

My father did not express an opinion, my mother definitely preferred marriage. She saw I was depressed because we were not able to resolve things; she came out with words that she probably regretted later: "If he doesn't want a marriage, you can still have a big celebration."

How simple and right that was: all in all the ritual repulsed me, too. Not to mention the fact that I had spent a number of years trying to not be "the daughter of"; then when I worked as a secretary I had spent other years acquiring a last name. With an identity that was finally pieced back together, I was not about to become "the wife of."

We received gifts, we organized a big reception: the non-wedding reception.

Massimo arrived a little late, causing me to go through the classic bride's panic of being left at the altar.

My mother pulled out all the crystal, my father sang anarchist songs with us (". . . the prostitutes / they are our daughters . . .") and I saw that he was happy.

A lot of people came: friends, relatives, acquaintances, but not Massimo's parents. Our decision was still too difficult for them to swallow, it made them too uncomfortable, and they didn't feel like condoning with their presence something that seemed to them so disrespectful of the family and its conventions.

Love can sometimes cause otherwise unthinkable leaps of faith: my mother-in-law was present in spirit with her splendid, sumptuous, famous *cassata*.

GIN FIZZ

juice of 1 lemon
1 t. sugar
1 vermouth-glass of gin
1 slice lemon
crushed ice

Someone gave me a heavy, pretentious shaker that I never use. So I limit myself to mixing carefully with a spoon, and I find the results quite acceptable.

In the world of cinema, the wave of 1968 was long, and no more ambiguous than elsewhere.

In 1972 the wave was still riding high, and the Italian Film Festival counter-festival in Venice met with success and recognition: the Biennale was a fiasco because the filmmakers pulled their films: we had won. My kingdom was the ditto machine; the smell of power kept in check the otherwise unbearable aching in my soul. The great directors wore blue jeans and licked stamps.

In so much unity and unanimity there were also those who made mistakes: a woman, who, after finally having made the film she had thought about for years left it to Brunello Rondi. She did so uncomfortably I imagine, but clearly determined not to miss her chance for the big screen.

The pages of the newspapers were full of the protest at Campo Santa Margherita, and the opening of her film at the Lido was greeted mainly by silence.

A month later, in Pesaro, we were still the same, a bit lost. The New Cinema Exhibition had already made its own revolution, and the push to act together and stay together took the form of marathon movie and eating sessions.

One evening, as a large number of us entered a pub (there were always a lot of us, going out in anything but a big group was unthinkable), there she was at a table, with her dog. Conspicuously we sat elsewhere, and until she left there was a constant exchange of caustic remarks about her, her film, her dog, her private life. We had chosen the right side of the barricade.

I too did my share, making ironic remarks about her white-tiled kitchen, and about the gin fizz that she had offered me the previous year when, one muggy night, I had dropped by her house to collect a signature. It had been a kind gesture toward a secretary, or toward a woman, or perhaps toward a human being.

TANGERINES

The papers wrote about my father's death.

At the beginning there was no pain, only relief for the end of his suffering, a feeling of resignation in the face of that last attempt that perhaps could have been made, but at what price: a definite feeling of guilt for that relief.

There was also much weariness, the standing for hours, the greeting of people that I could not always identify, the introductions, the customary phrases, the emotions of others, the organization of practical tasks that could not be avoided.

I didn't dress in black, but inevitably the question of whether to do so did arise. I counted the wreaths, the red banners, the honor guards. At the end of the day I would count the signatures in the guest book: this tallying up gives me a sense of security in any event, and I derive cabalistic formulas from it.

I worried that I did not have the appropriate demeanor, at least judging by the scowls of some of the visitors. Umberto Terracini on the other hand arrived cheerful, took the stairs, paused before the casket with the smile of one who has been face to face with death so many times—and with the daily habits of old age—so that he no longer fears it.

For three days I reentered, by hereditary right, into the great world of politics and culture. Behind the glass shelves in the imposing halls of the Cervi Institute, which my father had established and to which he had donated his library, the books that until that moment had lived in our home, changed image. I looked up the much-loved Nigra: the sticker with the catalog number affixed to the red leather binding gave it an entirely different physiognomy.

So many hands to shake, not all of them pleasant.

My mother was closed inside an armor of normality. I couldn't help her; indeed, I began to discover that I no longer felt legitimately her daughter.

The day of the funeral, springtime exploded over Rome: the spring of the protests and demonstrations. The previous week was March 12: it was raining hard and cars were burning in Largo Argentina. Massimo and I had sought shelter in a doorway, and outside the echoes of a war even reached the room where my father was lying in state.

At three in the afternoon, during the funeral eulogy, the sun beat hard on my gray Loden coat, on my suddenly-tight boots. My eyes were clouded by pollen, I feared a sudden attack of hay fever: small worries—my sore feet, the microphone balanced on a beer crate, the ashes of a Great Love demurely behind the hearse of a Great Leader and not even a gesture for me—distracted me from the speeches. I observed the chromatic effects of the "Historic Compromise,"[2] no red banner on the casket, no red flowers near it. The colors of the flag, nuances ranging from pink, to yellow, to violet, even on the wreath sent by President Leone, already on the brink of impeachment.[3]

We returned from the cemetery by taxi; mourning posters lined the streets, on the driver's seat the newspaper lay opened to the obituary. Public attention dulls internal tremors.

For three days we had in fact skipped meals; at home there was the empty place at the dinner table to face. We decided to have dinner in one of those places where you don't order, they automatically bring you what there is, and you don't have to think about it.

A family reunion with something festive about it. Maybe it was the spring air, maybe it was because we are not used to convivial reunions, maybe because from a family dressed in mourning one does not expect an outing to a restaurant.

By the end of the meal we were somewhat close to being cheerful: with the coffee, they brought us tiny stemmed glasses filled with tangerine juice.

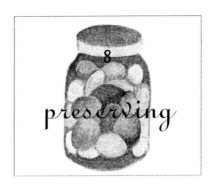

8

preserving

PICKLED GREEN BEANS

tender green beans
vinegar
garlic
tarragon
salt

I clean the string beans and cook them in a small amount of boiling salted water. When they are half cooked, I drain them, dry them with a cloth, and place them in glass jars. I warm the vinegar with the chopped garlic and the tarragon. I allow the mixture to cool and cover the string beans with it. Then I have only to seal the jars, and let them sit for at least a week.

MARINATED STRING BEANS

small string beans
vinegar
garlic
oil
salt

I cook the beans in equal amounts of water and vinegar (but just a little of each), with a good handful of salt. When they are still quite firm I drain them and dry them, then I place them in jars, adding small pieces of garlic here and there. I cover the beans with oil, shaking the jar a bit to allow air bubbles to surface, then I seal the jars.

PICKLED ONIONS

pearl onions

vinegar

I always buy the onions already cleaned, to avoid the craziness of doing it myself. I take the onions and arrange them in a jar (raw!), I cover them with vinegar, and leave them to steep for at least two weeks.

I am unable to reconstruct the breaking point. Up to a certain time in my life my father is a distant and stern image, but at the same time a safe one, affectionate, warm. For example, in our camping days (the war was still recent, so we used military tents, and everything from the oil lamps to the water skins had the insignia of some army or another), in that period we were still close. I would give him canteens full of blueberries, and we would call to each other from one thicket to another, with our own familiar "call of the wild."

Maybe it was when we moved. Aunt Ermelinda and the piano disappeared from my horizon—a relief. Other things disappeared as well: my schoolmates, the tangerines and walnuts in our garden, the big New Year's parties with a distinctive international flavor. The courtyard of Viale XXI Aprile (exploring the cellars, the goldfish pond, the enormous wisteria plant that was as good as a fortress) was replaced by a big garden bordered by the open countryside.

It was clear to me that this luxuriant and demanding territory did not belong to me.

An assiduous reader of *Little Men* and *The Pedagogic Poem*,[1] I had often built myself short-term vegetable gardens, windmills, and irrigation canals, just one way among many to play with water.

Fantasies of disappearance and omnipotence cohabitated in the fascination exercised upon me by survival skills. I knew *Mysterious Island* by heart. Everyone said I was a big girl now, and my father allotted me about fifteen square meters of land near the fence. He bought me a hoe and a shovel, and gave me a crash course in agronomy: he expected that I act with the same scientific-mindedness that he applied to political work, cultural work, even to his personal life. In France, during the war, his degree in agronomy and his own two arms had served him well in creating, along with all the intellectuals, a model farm and the best crops of the area. Days spent planting cabbages and potatoes, and nights planning the Unified Pact of Action.[2]

He came back from a trip to Japan full of ideas and books: he made my mother learn *ikebana*, he equipped the garden with rocks, gradients, and a puddle of water called "the pond," in which, during the summer, frogs and mosquitoes battled noisily.

My garden was not scientific: dahlias and tomatoes, eggplant and feijoa, Canterbury bells, beans, and peppers. A farmer would give me the seedlings, and sometimes I would weed: Pliny was more congenial to me than Columella. My father would come by occasionally to have a look, as he had done for the piano. He would raise his eyebrows, and predict a dismal future for my plantings if I did not follow his advice.

I did not, in fact, follow it, and my vegetables and flowers flourished: together with the farmers' daughters I ate some of the peppers, roasted on the coals, and sold the rest to my mother.

Those were the best years of her life: mistress of a daughter and a home that were finally hers, without Rebeccas behind every door, my mother was thriving and cheerful, ready to occupy those spaces that my father would gradually close off from the world. The big new two-story house sanctioned each person's solitude, and its distance from the city imposed long stays on everyone. My disorientation was only temporary, and solitude became my own realm too.

I soon abandoned the piece of land my father had entrusted to me. I took possession of an old pigsty that became "the hut." I built a fireplace, I set out chairs and a cot covered with a quilt. There I entertained my high-school friends and experienced my first limited sexual encounters. I planted dahlias and beans in the troughs that were now half-buried, I cooked peppers in the fireplace: my first house.

The occasions in which I was called upon to reconfirm family bonds began growing burdensome: outings, when at a restaurant my father would force on me the foods he thought to be the finest (fish chowder or game); Stefania, the little sister I had to babysit, who had all the things I never had; the Christmas gifts; the meals.

Gone were the social events—encounters with political and intellectual figures—either relocated to other sites or cancelled, and the only visitors now were Giulia's friends and my schoolmates.

In the garden, at the end of the summer, my mother became the intermediary for the only relationship possible: a passion for preserving drew me to her like a magnet, as I collaborated in the canning of fruit, tomatoes, marinated eggplant and peppers, and olives. I lined up the jars in a closet under the stairs, which was set up as a pantry, and my father inspected them complacently before shutting himself in his study again. In his own way he had brought to life his dream of "a little house in the country."

TOMATOES

firm San Marzano tomatoes
salt

I cut the tomatoes into chunks, add a little salt, and let them drain for an hour in a colander. Then I put them through the food mill fitted with a large-holed disk so that the skins will pass through along with the pulp. I place the purée in jars or bottles that seal, then wrap the containers in newspaper (they mustn't touch each other) and put them in a pot of cold water to cook. I bring the pot to a boil, and after twenty minutes I turn off the burner leaving the containers in the water until cool.

MARINATED EGGPLANT OR PEPPERS

purple eggplant or yellow and red peppers
kosher salt
vinegar
vegetable oil
parsley
garlic

I cut the eggplant (or peppers) into thin strips—without peeling them—and leave them to steep, with a couple of handfuls of salt in a soup tureen. After twenty-four hours I remove the liquid that has formed, cover them with vinegar, and let steep for another twenty-four hours. I dry the strips after having squeezed the water out of them, then I arrange them in small glass canning jars, adding garlic and parsley here and there. When the jar is full I add enough oil to cover.

FRUIT PRESERVES

I wash the fruit carefully (it must be very ripe), dry it, and remove cores, pits, seeds, and bruised parts.

I arrange the fruit in about one-and-a-half-inch layers, alternating with a half-inch layer of sugar. At the top I put a slightly thicker layer of sugar. I cover the top of the jar (which must not be more than three-quarters full) with a cloth, and I leave the jar in the sun for forty days. I then seal the jar, and leave it closed for at least three or four months: the longer I leave it, the more the fruit will ferment.

I serve these preserves as a dessert just as it is, or with a bit of whipped cream. Mostly though, I use them in preparing the Christmas cake.

We have our first real vacation in many years, certainly since before Tommaso's birth (and he's now five and a half). Back home again, all three of us struggle to return to our routines: the noise is intolerable to us, and we drag through shiftless, lazy days. Tommaso firmly declares that he does not wish to return to school; Massimo is unable to work.

A morning that still feels like summer; all three of us at the open market, laden with kilos of fruits and vegetables. I lead the shopping with a facade of confidence, keeping at bay a slight sense of guilt: now what am I going to do with all this. . . .

Massimo in a plastic apron, his glasses slipping down his nose, churns the food mill and squirts tomato juice on his beard, but he laughs. It sometimes happens that we too can play at being a family. Tommaso looks at us puzzled, and runs around sucking on a lemon wedge.

Lunch is at one, and shortly after three everything is already put away: jars of tomatoes are boiling in two enormous kettles (it's certainly not a necessity; probably they cost less at the supermarket. I use the excuse that it's for a special sauce for Tommaso and his schoolmates).

The tureens full of eggplant and peppers are something of an inconvenience; I'll have them underfoot for two days, but I tell myself that they will come in handy during the winter, in some of our many scantier suppers. On the terrace, in the sun, the fruit dominates in a large vase.

The kitchen shelf quakes under the weight of the jars: their colors, their irregularities and imperfections make them my own.

I am safe for at least one more winter.

DRIED BEEF

rump roast
kosher and regular salt
pepper

I cut the meat in 1/2-inch strips approximately, leaving whatever fat there is, and indeed, making sure that every strip has some. I then arrange it in a tureen, with plenty of both kosher and regular salt under and over the strips: the salt absorbs the blood and dries the meat. After twenty-four hours I remove the meat, leaving only a light coating of salt, and I rub all sides with pepper. I make a hole in every piece, and pass a string through each, with which I will hang the meat in a cool and well-ventilated space.

Most important (and most difficult) element: in order for the dried beef to turn out well there must be a northerly wind for at least the first three or four days (naturally this meat can only be prepared during the coldest winter days). The meat can be eaten as early as a week later, although a few more days will make it drier and easier to cut.

Grandmother Alfonsa's dried beef was like Aunt Ermelinda's *vov*: her masterpiece.

In the maid's room there was a wall closet made from what had been a French door. The upper part of the exterior wall was sealed and used as a pantry; the lower part had a grate in the outer wall that allowed air to circulate. There were wires strung across the inside of the closet for the drying of the meat. The strips of meat were wrapped in gauze darkened with pepper, and it always seemed to me that they continually oozed blood. There was something macabre about them that inevitably reflected on Grandmother Alfonsa, always there to make sure that the north wind did not dry them too much, or that the Sirocco did not darken or soften them.

My father loved those small, irregularly shaped red slices so much that he never insisted too much that I eat them. Maybe for this reason I had little trouble reclaiming them. Nonetheless I needed catalysts—my father's death and Tommaso's birth so close together—for this kosher food to enter full-fledged into my home-makerness, into the nostalgic and creative desire for a world in which, as Aunt Ermelinda used to say, "everything has its place, and every place its thing."

PRIMAVERA SAUCE

    8 plum tomatoes
    1 clove garlic
    6 basil leaves
    oil
    salt

This sauce is completely uncooked, so it can only be kept in the freezer: but it's so convenient, a few seconds in the food processor and right onto the pasta, to recreate summer in the coldest heart of winter.

VINEGAR

I have a big bottle without a hermetic seal in which I put, in the beginning, good-quality wine and various herbs: from parsley to cloves, from cumin to garlic to rosemary, all in minimal quantities, together with a very small amount of store-bought vinegar. Occasionally I add leftover wine (white or red) and infinitesimal amounts of aromatic herbs.

Between 1976 and 1977 Massimo was thinking about a documentary on Matteo Salvatore, imprisoned for homicide in San Marino. He read everything he could find, he listened to all his records again, and had me tell him what I knew. But this was not enough, he needed to speak with someone who knew Salvatore well: I suggested he meet with Giovanna.

I had to insist a great deal: he liked her music but he found her harsh, standoffish, at times intellectualistic; perhaps he was bothered too by the way in which I always held her up almost as a monument to a past of mine that Massimo had not shared and did not love.

Finally we went: she lived outside the city; there was a vegetable garden and fields next to the house.

Massimo sat on the edge of his chair, reluctant and timid; I too felt awkward. We talked about films and about ourselves, about her concern with the new record, and about politics. It got dark and she asked us to stay for dinner.

Massimo was completely won over by this sweet, fierce woman whose intelligence moves me. (I even felt a pang of jealousy sprout anew; how could I forget the repeated nightmares in which Giovanna used to reproach me: "Be quiet you, you have a tin ear.")

The country salad was full of aromatic herbs, drawn together by an extraordinary vinegar. A rich vinegar: she had gotten the starter from certain Piedmontese farmers when she was working in that area with the researchers of *Nuovo Canzoniere*.

She was too much "Mother" and "Creator" for me to have the courage to ask her for some of her vinegar: but I have managed to recreate it, more or less.

Now it happens, at times, that I offer someone a little of my vinegar: but it has to be someone special, because the vinegar reveals so much of me that it borders on the indiscreet.

WILD CHERRIES

2 lbs. wild cherries
2 lbs. sugar

I wash the wild cherries, remove the pits, and allow them to dry thoroughly. I then arrange them in a glass jar, alternating layers of cherries with layers of sugar.

I secure a piece of cloth around the mouth of the jar to close it, then I set the jar in the sun for forty days. Then I seal it hermetically and store it away for no less than three months.

Privileged destination: crepes.

Aunt Ermelinda used her own kitchen, more spacious and better equipped than ours though it was, only to make her morning coffee, which she prepared with her Neapolitan coffee pot, watchful for even the smallest splatter of coffee on the perfect white of her stove. The square tiles were always spotless and aseptic, and the only smell wafting in the air was that of pumice.

Except when we made the special-occasion semolina dumplings, and the odyssey of the *vov*, her strong egg liqueur. On those occasions, all the spaces were utilized, with the stream of straw-bottomed wine bottles to wash, the enormous white tureen, the specially-shaped ladles, and the sieve. The laborious operation lasted several days, and at the end the filled bottles were lined up in all their domestic majesty in the hall cupboard, next to the jars of wild cherries.

The credenza was dark and shiny, saturated with a multitude of aromas.

Muttering about the inefficiency of modern-day help, Aunt Ermelinda tidied up the kitchen, while with my finger I wiped up the last remnants from the white bowl. The recipe for *vov* has since been lost, and in any case I doubt that on my own I would be willing to go through Aunt Ermelinda's strenuous *tours de force* again. But the scent of that cupboard has returned in my own shelf, and it warms me.

The smells, the colors. The obsessions. The small sources of warmth are necessary to me, all of them, just as much as the large ones: for even adding them together I am no longer able to convince myself that my life is that dream that I had dreamed.

Who knows: perhaps even my father in the end had come to believe less in the Communist slogan, "The Sun of the Future," or to believe in a different way. Surely many stitches in the fabric had come undone, and I was one of the many. My improvisations with life, my struggle to survive, and his scientific method, his suicide by silence, an open war that spared no one until the very end.

He did not win. I limit myself to living.

MILK ELIXIR

1 qt. of milk
1 qt. of alcohol for making liqueurs

2 lbs. of sugar
3 t. vanilla extract
1 lemon

I cut the lemon into small pieces (all of it, rind as well as pulp) and I put it in a large bottle together with all the other ingredients: it is better to dissolve the sugar first in some warm milk. I seal the bottle hermetically and leave it there for two weeks, during which time I simply shake it two or three times a day.

When the two weeks are up I take a pan or a bowl on which I put a colander in which I have set a tight-weave cloth napkin. I pour the contents of the bottle into the napkin-covered colander and leave it, as the filtering of the liquid is a lengthy process.

The liquor will filter into the pan, and this of course will be poured into bottles and aged. A thick, yogurt-like cream, sweet-smelling and high in alcoholic content, will remain in the napkin. This can be stored in small jars, and eaten with a spoon.

LEMON VERBENA LIQUEUR

100 verbena leaves, picked during the month of June
20 fl. oz. of alcohol for liqueurs
17 oz. of sugar
5 cloves
a few pieces of cinnamon stick
1 qt. of water

I put the cinnamon stick, cloves, and verbena leaves in the alcohol, and let them steep for forty days, at the end of which I prepare a syrup by dissolving the sugar in the water, heated. I let the syrup cool, and mix with the alcohol from which I have removed the spices and leaves.

BITTER

1 handful of gentian flowers and roots
10 fl. oz. alcohol
17 oz. sugar
rind of one lemon

1 envelope powdered vanilla (or 1 t. extract)

1 qt. of water

I caramelize the sugar, then dissolve it in the water. I add the gentian and lemon peel and let it boil for about twenty minutes. I remove it from the heat, allow it to cool, filter it, and add the alcohol and vanilla, stirring well.

When my father died, a friend wrote to me that I had to accept the fact that I was no longer a daughter, and that I should bring all recriminations and vindications to a halt: I had only myself to take it out on.

The Adversary was no longer before me, and now I no longer had roots, at least as far as the official records were concerned.

Then I realized that I could stop killing myself, I could even allow myself to have enough happiness to give to others, to make my own roots. Tommaso was born, and the responsibility of having him sometimes weighs on me so heavily that I need to dilute it by diverting it. I try to keep the world at bay with small devices, disjointed survival strategies in order to bind people and things to me.

Though I try to dig my roots inside myself, I obstinately depend on the outside, on people and things that are unable to guarantee my security. So the home—habit, solitude, negritude—becomes an absorbent and flamboyant root: I cannot leave it to itself, I cannot abide the disorder, the dust, the empty flower vase. So I have a cleaning woman twice a week: the big things are taken care of, I no longer do the heavy work. But so many small gestures remain—empty the ashtrays, plump the sofa cushions, pick up Tommaso's toys, water the plants on the terrace, stack the magazines, turn off the bathroom water heater when I turn the washer on or the fuse will blow, cook and host, buy milk, clean the oil cruet at least once in a while, put sets of clothing away with the changing seasons, separate whites from darks before putting clothes in the washer, hang them on the line and take them down, wash the curtains, take them down, put them back up, sew on buttons, dust the pictures or else why bother hanging them, buy fertilizer for the plants, weatherstrip the windows, put a new roll of toilet paper on the holder, clean the filter on the dishwasher, buy replacement batteries for Tommaso's toys, remove the calcium deposits from the coffee pot and the iron, buy one detergent for cotton and another for wool, silk, nylon, extra-strong paper towels and a new needle for the turntable, kosher salt and table salt, slice the roast, grate the Parmesan cheese: curb the foul smells, the deterioration, the shattering—without these gestures one can't survive; I can't survive.

Because I can't stand to serve just a pan-cooked cutlet and salad (which in any case would mean shopping almost every day), because a purely functional life is intolerable without small luxuries, without a bit of special attention, without a little extravagance.

And so my aerial self sinks into the jars, into the liqueurs, into the potted plants on the terrace, into the sweaters and blankets with which I would like to ensnare the world, into the freezer. Because in my life, pieced together with ill-fitting bits, in the mosaic of my life (as in everyone's, but more so women's) keeping house can also mean a little warm place.

A small corner that is constantly changing, for its stillness would mean death, and recipes are only a base on which to build new flavors, new combinations every time.

Reinventing is the only possible way to escape our boundaries, reinventing so as not to tread over the same ground, reinventing so as not to eat one's heart out. Everything has already been said, everything has already been written:

> [. . .] Let us not forget, at any rate, that at the end of the eighteenth century the evolution of the Neapolitans from "leaf-eaters" to "macaroni-eaters"—if it may be considered complete—has not yet, however, been crowned (so to speak) by that which to us, today, appears as an essential and integral element of that evolution. The macaroni of which Goethe speaks in his *Journey through Italy*, in fact, and most likely the same one toward which Leopardi directed his satire, when in his poem *The New Believers* he proclaimed:
>
> > [. . .] Naples takes up arms, its macaroni to defend;
> > And it's for the macaroni that they fight until the end.
> > They cannot understand

When macaroni tastes so good,
Why towns and provinces and countries,
Are not made happy by this food.

—that macaroni, as I was saying, was still, let us not forget, in the early decades of the nineteenth century, macaroni flavored *only with grated cheese*, or, at best, with a meat gravy. It was only around 1830, it seems, that a sauce with tomato (and then with a tomato paste), which today appears to us so typical and essential for this dish—became widespread among the Neapolitan population.

But this is another story, one that may even be worth investigating at another time, with all the philological and historiography rigor that it deserves. It does, however go beyond the picture of the investigation that we have set before us, concerning the evolution of the Neapolitans from "leaf-eaters" to "macaroni-eaters:" therefore, to those who would ask us why Neapolitans began to flavor their pastas with tomato, we would provisionally answer—for once—that "the spirit will flutter where it will."

(E. Sereni, "Notes on the History of Nutrition in Southern Italy: Neapolitans, From 'Leaf Eaters' to 'Macaroni Eaters,'" *New Land and Red Cattle*, Turin, 1981).

Notes

INTRODUCTION

1. See Doreen Carvajal's breezy overview of this production in her article "Be Thankful This Isn't a Story about Cannibalism," *New York Times*, 16 November 1997.

2. The utopian spirit of the organization spearheaded by Sereni is amply stated in the auspicious choice of the same name of 17th-century philosopher's Tommaso Campanella famous utopian work *La città del sole* (The City of the Sun), one of the most enduring theoretical visions of a pragmatic and spiritual communist society.

3. Personal statement of Clara Sereni in a bio blurb sent to me.

4. In his book, *The Flavors of Modernity*, Biasin paraphrases Hans Blumemberg's concept of "reading" the world through the "reading" of food and nutritional habits (Biasin, 27).

5. Here it appears significant to pair the character of Concezione in Vittorini's *Conversazione in Sicilia* with Sereni's grandmother Alfonsa, two women very possibly of the same generation, in seemingly timeless features and postures. Alfonsa, like Concezione, is a no-nonsense woman who wears men's shoes, and even though she is not remembered as a great cook, her food, like her presence, evokes basic sustenance to the narrator.

6. See Marialisa Calta's article "Take a Novel, Add a Recipe, and Season to Taste," *New York Times*, 17 February 1993.

7. Ibid.

8. For a discussion on the discourse of feminism and femininity focused around representations of caring practices and food preparation, see Miceli Jeffries "Caring and Nurturing in Italian Women's Theory and Fiction: A Reappraisal," in *Feminine Feminists: Cultural Practices in Italy*.

9. Recorded interview with Clara Sereni in Rome, July 1990.

10. For an analysis of Sereni's treatment of history as a discourse between the personal and the public, see Miceli Jeffries "Unsigned History: Silent, Micro Technologies of Gender in the Narratives of the Quotidian," in *Gendering Italian Fiction.*

11. In their analysis of *Casalinghitudine*, Mirna Cicioni and Susan Walker refer to Sereni's "autobiographical persona" as the constructed self of an "autobiographical fiction." They see in the fragmented structure of the book a subversive attempt on the part of the author to demolish the notion of a specific relational identity (37–38).

12. An example of this is the frequency with which the Italian verb *sconfinare*, which both means to go over/beyond the border and to trespass, appears in both her fiction and nonfiction writing. The Italian verb and the noun *sconfinamento* evoke in their sound a sense of spaciousness and movement that cannot be replicated in the English translation (*Conversazione con Clara Sereni*, 8) [Conversation with Clara Sereni].

13. Stephen Gundle's *Between Hollywood and Moscow* offers an articulated and spirited analysis of the political and cultural history of the Italian Communist Party since the Second World War (19).

14. In her essay "Recipes for Reading," Susan Leonardi examines the reproducibility and sharing of recipes. "Like a narrative," she writes, "a recipe is reproducible, and, further, its hearers-readers-receivers are encouraged to reproduce it and, in reproducing it, to revise it and make it their own. Unlike the repetition of a narrative (folktales, ghosts stories), however, a recipe's reproducibility can have a literal result, the dish itself" (344).

15. On more than one occasion in the book, the narrator is quite candid about her attraction to the "scent of riches," the "red thread" that runs through her life that generates desires for beautiful and superfluous possessions, an undercurrent that at various times is neutralized by her conscious rejection of material acquisitions (140).

16. In this regard, Giuliana Menozzi, in her article "Food and Subjectivity in Clara Sereni's *Casalinghitudine*," observes that "the narrator learns that autonomy lies outside the family which she soon leaves, and in creating her own recipes, a skill she comes to perfect" (222). Menozzi's analysis of the book centers on the mediating aspect of the food as the narrator negotiates her way between autonomy and dependence by acquiring knowledge of herself.

CHAPTER 1

1. The term refers to soft puréed food, most often baby food. It is also a 'baby talk' term used to signify a meal.

CHAPTER 2

1. The so-called Swindle Law was a 1952 Italian law stipulating that a single political party or a coalition of parties obtaining 50% + 1 of the general electoral vote, would automatically have the majority of seats in Parliament. The law was highly contested by the Communist Party and never became effective.

2. This is a reference to the University of Trento in Northeast Italy, where the department of sociology became a hotbed of theoretical political debate and organized protests during the student movement in 1968. These were the beginnings of national student unrest.

CHAPTER 3

1. Location of the headquarters of the Italian Communist Party in Rome.

2. Pear shaped tomatoes grown in the area around Naples, well known for their sweetness.

3. Traditional Sicilian layered cake, see recipe in "Sweets" chapter.

4. International Communist Organization.

5. Maremma is an area of the coastal plains of Tuscany.

6. Commonly sold in Italian grocery stores, it is a lightly salted cheese which is briefly baked in order to make it more dry.

7. A very flavorful, somewhat aged farmer cheese typical of Tuscany and the surrounding areas.

CHAPTER 4

1. Pejorative slang, used among the Italian Jews.

2. In Italian, *dragoncello* also means "little dragon."

CHAPTER 5

1. Rossana Rossanda, Italian feminist activist, and Luigi Pintor, head of the Italian Communist Party.

CHAPTER 7

1. A snack cake on the order of Hostess Cakes.

2. The Historic Compromise which took place in 1973, refers to a shift in the Communist Party policy. It sought an alliance with the Christian Democratic Party in the name of the greater political good.

3. In '75 a political scandal shook the Christian Democrat cabinet as several ministers were accused of having accepted bribes from the American company Lockheed. The crisis culminated with the resignation of President Giovanni Leone.

CHAPTER 8

1. A work by Russian writer A.S. Makarenko.

2. The Unified Pact of Action (Patto d'Unità d'Azione) was a unified action plan of various leftist resistance groups that eventually formed the Popular Front Party.

Works Cited

Barolini, Helen. *Festa. Recipes and Recollections of Italian Holidays.* Madison: University of Wisconsin Press, 1988, 2002.

Biasin, Gian-Paolo. *The Flavors of Modernity.* Princeton: Princeton University Press, 1993.

———. "Italo Calvino in Mexico: Food and Lovers, Tourists and Cannibals." *PMLA* 108.1 (1993): 72–88.

Calta, Marialisa. "Take a Novel, Add a Recipe, and Season to Taste." *New York Times*, 17 February 1993.

Carvajal, Doreen. "Be Thankful This isn't a Story about Cannibalism." *New York Times*, 16 November 1997.

Cicioni, Mirna and Susan Walker. "Picking up the Pieces: Clara Sereni's Recipes for Survival." In *Novel Turns Toward 2000: Critical Perspectives on Contemporary Narrative Writing from Western Europe*, edited by John Gatt-Rutter, 35–47. Victoria (Australia): Voz Hispanica, 2000.

Ehlrich, Elizabeth. *Miriam's Kitchen: A Memoir.* New York: Penguin Books, 1998.

Gaglianone, Paola and Giorgio Luti, eds. *Conversazione con Clara Sereni, Donne, Scrittura, Politica.* Rome: Omicron, 1990.

Gundle, Stephen. *Between Hollywood and Moscow.* Durham: Duke University Press, 2000.

Heat-Moon, William Least. *PrairyErth.* Boston: Houghton Mifflin, 1991.

Leonardi, Susan J. "Recipes for Reading." PMLA 3 (1989): 340–347.

Menozzi, Giuliana, "Food and Subjectivity in Clara Sereni's *Casalinghitudine.*" *Italica* 71, 2 (1994): 217–227.

Miceli Jeffries, Giovanna. "Caring and Nurturing in Italian Women's Theory and Fiction: A Reappraisal." In *Feminine Feminists: Cul-*

tural Practices in Italy, 87–108. Edited by Giovanna Miceli Jeffries. Minneapolis: University of Minnesota Press, 1994.

———. "Unsigned History: Silent, Micro Technologies of Gender in the Narratives of the Quotidian." In *Gendering Italian Fiction*, 71–84. Edited by Maria Ornella Marotti and Gabriella Brooke. Cranbury, (N.J.): Associated University Presses, 1999.

———. "La tensione civile nella narrativa di Clara Sereni." In *Studi in onore di Umberto Mariani: da Verga a Calvino*, 187–198. Edited by Anthony G. Costantini and Franco Zangrilli. Firenze: Edizioni Cadmo, 2000.

Parati, Graziella. *Public History, Private Stories: Italian Women's Auto-biography*, Minneapolis: University of Minnesota Press, 1996.

Reichl, Ruth. *Tender at the Bone.* New York: Random House, 1998.

Roden, Claudia. *The Book of Jewish Food.* New York: A. Knopf, 1996.

Sargisson, Lucy. "Contemporary Feminist Utopianism." In *Literature and the Political Imagination*, 238–255. Edited by John Horton and Andrea T. Baumeister. London and New York: Routledge, 1996.

Shange, Ntozake. *Sassafras, Cypress & Indigo.* New York: St. Martin Press, 1982.

Vittorini, Elio. *Conversation in Sicily.* Translated by Wilfrid David. Harmonsworth: Penguin, 1961.

Wolf, Marjery. "Always an Outsider." Conference given at the Women Studies Research Center, University of Wisconsin, Madison, February 27, 1998.